The Movie Novel

Robots: The Movie Novel

First published in the USA by HarperKids Entertainment in 2005

First published in Great Britain by HarperCollinsEntertainment 2005

HarperCollinsEntertainment is an imprint of HarperCollins Publishers Ltd,

77-85 Fulham Palace Road, Hammersmith, London W6 8JB

www.robotsmovie.com

www.harpercollinschildrensbooks.co.uk

ISBN 0-00-719224-X

1 2 3 4 5 6 7 8 9 10

The Movie Novel

by Nancy Krulik

■ HarperCollins*Entertainment*
An imprint of HarperCollinsPublishers

"**W**oo-hoo! I'm going to be a dad!" Herb Copperbottom shouted his big news as he ran through the streets of Rivet Town. He wanted the whole world to know how happy he was.

"I just talked to my wife. My baby is going to be delivered any minute!" He stopped in the middle of the street to tell a traffic cop.

The cop didn't seem particularly thrilled. Neither did the truck driver who had to slam on his brakes to avoid running over Herb Copperbottom.

"Hey, get out of the way!" the truck driver snarled.

But nothing could upset Herb today. He was going to be a

dad. He'd dreamed of this moment for a very long time. He raced through the streets, trying to get home before the baby came.

But he wasn't quick enough. When he arrived at his house, his wife gave him the news. "Oh, honey, I'm so sorry," Mrs. Copperbottom said. "You missed the delivery."

Herb's face fell. He'd missed it. The most important moment of his life, and he'd missed it.

"It's okay," Mrs. Copperbottom assured him. "Making a baby is half the fun." She reached out her arms and handed her husband a huge brown box. The words BUILD-A-BABY KIT were splashed across the side of it.

Mr. Copperbottom needed no further encouragement. He gingerly carried the box of parts into the dining room and carefully set it on the table. Then he reached over and purposefully began to open the carton. He removed each of the pieces of metal, the screws, joints, and nails that would soon become their very own son or daughter.

The Copperbottoms sat, working together, for the rest of the night. They acted as a team, studying the intricate directions that came in the box, placing cotter pins into small holes, using a wrench to tighten the bolts that held the tiny limbs in place, screwing on the child's metal skull, and popping its butt plate into place. It was difficult work for sure, but it was a labor of love.

Finally, after twelve tough hours, Mr. and Mrs. Copperbottom heard the sound they had waited for for so long.

"Waaaahhh!" Their baby son let out a wail. It was strong and powerful and not at all tinny.

Mrs. Copperbottom picked up her son and held his body close to hers. "Twelve hours of labor." She sighed, cradling him in her arms. "Oh, but it was worth it."

"Look at him," her husband added, with unbridled pride and joy. The baby was really cute, with a pointy metal plate on his shimmering sky blue forehead, two bright red ears, and a tiny, screw-shaped nose. All his parts were there. Ten tin fingers and ten tin toes. "Look! Look at how bright his eyes are. I don't know how I'm going to do it. But I'm going to see that he has everything he needs. I'll work nights."

Mrs. Copperbottom nodded encouragingly. She knew it would be tough raising a child on their limited means. After all, her husband was only a dishwasher at a local restaurant. A front-load dishwasher, yes, but certainly not the most modern model. Still, she had no doubt that somehow they would be able to raise this child to be a strong, proud robot. She smiled down at her son and gave him a wonderful robot name.

Rodney Copperbottom.

odney grew quickly. Every year on his birthday his parents presented him with a different carton filled with larger replacement parts. The Copperbottoms weren't wealthy robots, so none of Rodney's ever-growing parts were bright and shiny, like his original baby body parts. Rather, these parts were hand-me-downs, mostly from his cousin Jeffrey. But Mr. and Mrs. Copperbottom worked as best they could to clean up the metal, and they managed to get rid of most of the smell. With some minor adjustments, Rodney found he could make the parts fit well enough.

When Rodney was five years old, his father took him to a parade in the middle of town. The crowd was three rows deep, but Rodney, perched on his dad's shoulders, could see perfectly. A giant helium-filled balloon passed overhead. It was obviously patterned after the form of a very large robot—one with a rotund body, two long, spaghetti-like arms, and a small round head. Rodney couldn't take his eyes off the giant gray-and-yellow balloon as it floated by.

"Hey, Dad, who's that?" he asked excitedly.

"That, Rodney, is Bigweld. He's the greatest robot in the world."

Rodney seemed confused. "I thought you were the greatest robot in the world," he told his dad with great sincerity.

Mr. Copperbottom was so proud, he nearly burst a gasket. "Besides me," he corrected himself. Then he explained, "He's the head of Bigweld Industries. He invents things that make everyone's life better. He's a genius."

"Could I meet him?" the boy asked.

"Maybe someday."

Rodney was quiet for a moment, considering how cool it must be to invent things that help people. That started him wondering. "What do you do?" he asked his father.

"I work in a big fancy restaurant. I'm a dishwasher," Mr. Copperbottom told him proudly.

Rodney looked up at him in awe. Now he was sure his father was the greatest robot around.

Bigweld came a close second.

Rodney's fascination with inventing only grew as he got older. Every night he would watch The Bigweld Show on TV. The young bot danced around the room excitedly whenever he heard the show's theme song on the air. When the announcer shouted, "And now . . . the host of our show, Bigweld!" Rodney leaped up and down so excitedly, his mother sometimes thought he might pop a spring.

Rodney never tired of the show. He loved Bigweld's amazing charm. His voice was wise and kind. He built incredible things— and Rodney really loved watching him construct elaborate patterns with dominoes. Most important, Bigweld's never-ending encouragement was the stuff a young bot's dreams were made of.

Rodney's favorite episode was the one in which Bigweld gave the television audience a tour of his company headquarters in Robot City.

"Welcome!" Bigweld said from inside the TV. "This week, I thought you might like to take a look around Bigweld Industries." The huge robot pointed to a shimmering metal gate. "This here's the front gate. Kinda cute, isn't it?" He turned to the guard standing outside the gate. "Good morning, Tim."

"Good morning, Mr. Bigweld, sir," Tim the guard replied.

Mr. Bigweld looked at him curiously. "Tim, who closed the front gate?" he asked. "We never shut the gate. Shutting the gate means shutting out fresh ideas."

Rodney watched as the camera panned to a line of robots standing outside the gate. They were eagerly clutching blueprints and mechanical devices. Bigweld looked kindly at them and smiled out at the TV audience. "You see, every day, robots come from hither and yon, bringing us new ideas. And I listen to every one of 'em. Because you never know which young bot is going to change the world. Remember . . . whether a bot is made of new parts, old parts, or spare parts, you can shine no matter what you're made of."

Rodney grinned broadly. He was certain Bigweld was talking to him. He was destined to become an inventor! Bigweld's show was Rodney's great inspiration. He kept Bigweld's words in his head and in his heart.

"Why invent anything unless it makes someone's life better? So look around for a need, and start coming up with ideas to fill that need. One idea will lead to another, and before you know it, you've done it! See a need, fill a need!"

That was Rodney's goal. All he had to do was come up with something that had never been made before—something that could help other robots, and surely Mr. Bigweld would help him make his dreams a reality!

Rodney refused to give up on his dreams. Throughout the next few years, he kept working on his secret invention. He called it the Wonderbot.

The Wonderbot wasn't much to look at it. It was part old teapot, part metal spools, with a few spoons thrown in for good measure. But it was a highly technical mechanical invention, and although he wasn't quite sure what it would be used for, Rodney knew it would help robots live better lives. Despite the fact that right now the only thing it was good at was exploding, someday the Wonderbot would make Rodney shine. And Rodney definitely needed to shine.

As he grew older, his hand-me-down replacement parts became more worn and shabby. During one particularly embarrassing period of adolescence, he actually had to wear his cousin Veronica's hand-me-downs.

Yet Rodney never seemed to mind the old parts his parents gave him or the seemingly endless teasing of his classmates. He didn't need to be popular. His mind was set on a single goal—to get out of Rivet Town and make his way to Robot City. Once he got there, he knew he would change the world.

CHAPTER THREE

At the moment, the world around Rodney wasn't so wonderful. Now that he was eighteen, he was trying to earn a few extra dollars by working as a busboy at the same restaurant as his father. He hoped the money would help him get to Robot City. Being a busboy was hard work, but not nearly as hard as seeing his father humiliated. No matter how much the dishwasher tried, his boss, Mr. Gunk, wasn't satisfied with Mr. Copperbottom's job performance. He was determined to make Rodney's dad keep up with the newer, more improved dishwashers, even though there was no way Mr. Copperbottom could work faster without getting upgrades himself.

"Is it a contest to see how slow you can work?" Mr. Gunk

demanded of Rodney's dad. "'Cause you're winning. I told you fifty times: You're too slow. Get an upgrade!" He shoved five more dishes into Mr. Copperbottom's front-load stomach.

"Upgrades are very expensive, sir, and I . . . ," Mr. Copperbottom began.

But Mr. Gunk wasn't listening. He'd been distracted by a waiter who'd come running into the kitchen. "Mr. Gunk, a customer is choking," the waiter said excitedly.

Mr. Gunk sighed and grabbed a plunger from the closet. On his way out the door, Mr. Gunk spotted Rodney standing by the side of the room, watching. "What are you? On a break?" he demanded, before storming away to unclog his customer.

Rodney looked at his father's tired, browbeaten expression and simply had to do something to help. He picked up his small carrying case and pulled out the latest incarnation of his invention, the Wonderbot.

"Can I try it now, Dad?" he asked.

Mr. Copperbottom seemed unsure. "Maybe we should get Mr. Gunk's approval first," he suggested.

But Rodney was determined. He had faith that his invention could help his dad. "Let's just show him," he said excitedly.

"Come on, this is going to make your job easier. I invented it for you."

Rodney's enthusiasm was contagious. Mr. Copperbottom got caught up in the moment. "Okay, let's try it."

"Great!" the young robot exclaimed. He turned to the Wonderbot. "Okay, this is it," he told his invention. "Wonderbot, go to work!"

Instantly, the Wonderbot whirled its giant spoons like helicopter blades and soared over the heads of the kitchen crew. They ducked to avoid being decapitated. The Wonderbot didn't even seem to know they were there. It was too intent on studying the way Mr. Copperbottom washed dishes.

After a few moments, the Wonderbot got to work. It started out at a slow pace, grabbing a few dirty dishes, placing them inside Mr. Copperbottom's washing mechanism, and then removing, drying, and stacking them.

When Rodney was satisfied his invention had mastered the task, he gave the Wonderbot a thumbs-up. Instantly, the invention picked up the pace. In moments, it became its own assembly line, simultaneously loading, washing, removing, drying, and stacking.

The Wonderbot worked! It really worked! Rodney reached up his hand and gave his dad a high five.

The kitchen staff was plenty impressed, too. They stopped what they were doing to cheer the Wonderbot on.

That was all the encouragement Rodney's invention needed. It started really hamming it up, flipping the plates into the air, juggling, and spinning them.

"Yeah! Bravo!" the waiters shouted.

"Go, man! Whoa!" cried the floorwasher.

The Wonderbot moved even faster, getting all the dirty dishes and silverware washed and stacked so fast, it even had time to grab a doughnut and a cup of coffee.

The kitchen staff cheered wildly . . . until Mr. Gunk entered the room. "Copperbottom," the angry boss demanded. "What is that?"

The Wonderbot was frightened by Mr. Gunk's booming voice. It cowered in a corner.

Mr. Copperbottom stretched to stand as tall and proud as a dishwasher could. "My son made it."

"What's it doing?" The boss's voice roared loudly across the kitchen.

The Wonderbot whirred with fright.

"Mr. Gunk, please, you're making it nervous," Rodney pleaded.

"I want to know what it is!" he bellowed back, ignoring Rodney's warning.

Mr. Gunk's deep, loud voice echoed around the room. The Wonderbot was completely freaked out. The tiny invention let out an anguished wail, shook violently, and then blasted around the kitchen, bouncing like a giant Superball and smashing into anything that blocked its path.

Crash! Smash! Boom! Pieces of broken china flew around the kitchen.

"Look out!" members of the kitchen crew cried, as they ducked out of the way.

"It's wrecking my kitchen!" Mr. Gunk shouted. Then, taking matters into his own hands, he grabbed an axe and began chasing the wild Wonderbot. "I'll stop it!"

"No!" Rodney insisted, grabbing Mr. Gunk by the foot. The boss lost his balance and fell into a vat of slimy, smelly, disgusting liquid.

The Wonderbot wasn't about to wait around for Mr. Gunk to

emerge from that mess. It raced into the main dining room of the restaurant, flying frantically above the patrons' heads before zooming out the door.

Mr. Gunk heard screaming coming from the restaurant. He pulled himself out of the gross puddle and lunged for Mr. Copperbottom. "Your son, huh?" he bellowed.

Rodney leaped in front of his father and blocked Mr. Gunk's path. "It wasn't his fault," he insisted. "He had nothing to do with . . ."

But Mr. Copperbottom was still proud of his son. "Yes, sir, he is a brilliant boy. An inventor."

Mr. Gunk groaned. "Clean up this mess!" he ordered the old dishwasher. Then he turned to Rodney. "And you! Get out! Inventor . . ." He shook his head at the absurdity of it all. "You're the hand-me-down son of a dishwasher, and that's all you'll ever be." A group of restaurant patrons had gathered behind Mr. Gunk. Their laughter seconded the big boss's opinion.

But Rodney knew better. He'd show them. He'd show them all!

It didn't take Mr. and Mrs. Copperbottom long to find Rodney. Mrs. Copperbottom knew just where to look. Somehow she figured that her son had already packed up his wayward Wonderbot, gone to the train depot, and was about to purchase a one-way ticket to Robot City.

"I told you we'd find him," a very wound-up Mrs. Copperbottom boasted, as she raced through the depot toward her son. "It's a mother's instinct."

"Instinct?" Mr. Copperbottom huffed and puffed as he hurried behind her. "He left us a note. It said, 'I'm leaving, I'll be at the train station.'"

"Never mind," his wife replied. She grabbed Rodney and hugged him with relief. Then she frowned. "Pick up that suitcase," she said, scolding him as if he was five years old again. "You're coming home right now."

But Rodney no longer had five-year-old hand-me-down parts. He was made of adult metal now—and he'd steeled his mind to what he wanted to do.

"No, Mom," he replied firmly. "I have to do this. I'm going to Robot City. Tonight. I'm going to get a job, and I'm going to help Dad pay back Mr. Gunk."

Mrs. Copperbottom shot her husband an exasperated look. "Talk to him!" she pleaded.

"Uh . . . ," Mr. Copperbottom stalled.

It was obvious that Mrs. Copperbottom wasn't going to get any help there. "Robot City?" she demanded. "You're just a kid!"

"Mom, I just don't fit in here," Rodney explained, trying desperately to get her to understand.

"Nonsense!" his mother exclaimed. "Everybody in town loves you."

But before she could finish her sentence, she was drowned out by a newspaper bot shouting out the latest headline. "Extra! 'Idiot Busboy Destroys Restaurant. Humiliates Family.' Read all about it! Extra! Extra!"

Rodney sighed. "I'm never gonna be someone here. I want to be an inventor. I want to meet Bigweld. I want to be somebody."

"You are somebody. Somebody who's not getting on that train," she insisted.

"Yes, I am."

"No, you're not."

"Yes, I am."

Mrs. Copperbottom turned to her husband. "Talk to him."

The old dishwasher put his hand on his son's shoulder. "One ticket for Robot City," he said to the man behind the ticket counter.

Mrs. Copperbottom looked at him strangely. "Where are you going?" she demanded.

"Not me," her husband replied calmly. "Him."

"But . . ."

"He's right," Mr. Copperbottom continued. "In this town he'll always just be the son of a dishwasher." He turned to his son. "Rodney, did you know that when I was your age, I wanted to be a musician? I played pretty well, too. But my dad was worried that that I wouldn't be able to make a living. So they had me refitted to be a dishwasher. I'm not complaining, but I always said to myself that if I could do it over again, I would follow my dream. You've got greatness, Rodney. Never doubt it. You go to Robot City. You go meet Bigweld. And you show him your big ideas. And Rodney, never, never give up."

Rodney could feel the oil building up in his eyes. He blinked to keep himself from crying as the train pulled into the station. "All aboard!" the conductor shouted.

Mrs. Copperbottom grabbed her son and hugged him like she would never let him go. Finally, her husband had to pry her fingers apart and pull her away. Rodney raced off.

"I won't let you down, Dad," he vowed as he stood in the

23

doorway of the train. "I'll make you proud."

"I already am," Mr. Copperbottom replied, as the door closed and the train pulled out of the station.

CHAPTER FOUR

It wasn't a long journey to Robot City—it took no more than a few hours by train. But as Rodney stepped out of the huge train depot and onto the hustling, bustling sidewalk, he felt as though he'd traveled worlds away.

Rodney's small, quiet hometown was nothing like this. Compared to Rivet Town, Robot City seemed huge and imposing, with its tall skyscrapers and hundreds of bots hurrying by. But even though he was surrounded by bots, Rodney had never felt so alone. For a moment he wondered if he'd made a mistake.

Then he saw the sign.

WELCOME TO ROBOT CITY it proclaimed. Beneath the words was

a huge picture of Bigweld. No, Rodney hadn't made a mistake at all.

He headed into the subway station just below ground. He stopped by the token booth to ask directions from the train announcer. "Hi. Excuse me, how do I get to Bigweld Industries?"

"Hffgszmlrp."

The announcer's response was a completely garbled mess. "What?" Rodney asked.

The announcer pointed behind Rodney and repeated his muffled gibberish. Rodney turned around and saw a sign leading to the entrance of the Crosstown Express.

The Crosstown Express resembled an amusement park Ferris wheel. Rodney hopped into one of the podlike cars and immediately began moving slowly around the hub. A big smile flashed across his face. He was prepared to waltz right in and show Bigweld his invention. He was ready to shine.

The pod moved until it linked up with another just like it. A gangly red robot named Fender was fast asleep in the car next to him. He was sleeping so soundly, he was actually drooling. Gross!

Suddenly, the sleeping robot started to droop over. His head landed right on Rodney's shoulder. Rodney could feel the wet, oily drool landing on him. Yuck! Quickly, he tried to push the bot off of him. Unfortunately, instead of moving over, the bot fell right into Rodney's lap!

"What the, oh . . . are you following me?" Fender asked as he sat up, yawning.

"No!" Rodney answered, defensively.

"First time on the Crosstown Express?" Fender asked him.

"Well, actually I . . ." But Fender wasn't interested in what Rodney had to say.

"Whoo-boy! Well, good luck in the big city. If you make it here, you can make it anywhere. And if you can't make it here, welcome to the club."

As the pod neared the top of the tracks, Rodney gasped. He had his first wonderful view of the city from high up. It was an incredible sight. Chrome skyscrapers touched the clouds, while, down below, the bots and cars looked like tiny metallic ants. "Wow!" he exclaimed.

"Oh, no!" Fender gasped.

"What? What is it?" Rodney asked him nervously.

"We're going off the tracks. We're gonna crash!"

"What?" Rodney exclaimed. But his voice was drowned out

by the fast motion of the pod shooting down at a tremendous speed.

"Woo-hoo!" Fender shouted, as his head spun around backward. He quickly cracked his neck and returned his face to the correct side of his body. He smiled at Rodney. "I was just kidding," he told him.

Rodney breathed a sigh of relief.

"Now we're gonna die," Fender announced, as their vehicle fell into a catapult.

The catapult launched their pod into the air at top speed. The little pod pinged and ponged around in the air like a metal ball in a pinball machine! Rodney was petrified.

The red robot, however, seemed to be having a blast. Fender raised his arms up like he was riding a roller coaster as they zoomed through tunnels and over hills. Rodney was thrown against the side of the car. Then, Fender threw up.

Finally, the pod came to a stop. Rodney literally fell back into his seat, his body limp.

"You know," Fender reassured him, "it used to be a lot worse. They had this giant hammer . . ."

Just then, Rodney saw a huge hammer careening toward the

spot where their pod had come to rest.

"Oh, they brought it back," Fender had time to mutter before the hammer connected with the wall of their pod. Before Rodney knew what was happening, Fender's butt was in his face, as their pod spun wildly in tight circles.

When the pod finally stopped its mad spinning, Rodney was powerless against the returning force of gravity. He fell out the pod door and Fender stepped out beside him.

"Just stick with me, kid. I know this town like the back of my hand." Fender was just beginning another of his snooty speeches when, luckily for Rodney, the hammer returned and knocked Fender off into the city.

Rodney picked himself up off the ground and turned around. He was standing right in front of Bigweld Industries!

"Wow!" Rodney gasped as he approached the front gate of Bigweld Industries. It looked exactly the way it did on TV. He smiled excitedly as he spotted the familiar sign above the gate. It read YOU CAN SHINE NO MATTER WHAT YOU'RE MADE OF, and it was signed, "Bigweld."

Rodney's excitement increased as he recognized the guard in

front of the giant gate. It was Tim, the same guard who appeared on The Bigweld Show. Rodney stared at him for a moment, thrilled to be in his presence.

"Yoo-hoo." Tim interrupted Rodney's adoring stare. "Can I help you?"

"Sorry," Rodney murmured, startled by the sound of Tim's voice. "I . . . I . . . you're Tim from the TV show."

"That's me!" Tim replied.

"Well, hey, Tim! Who closed the front gate?" Rodney asked, repeating the words he'd heard Bigweld say so many times before. "It's never supposed to be—"

Tim sighed. He'd heard that line a million times before. "Yeah, okay," he interrupted Rodney. "What do you want?"

"I'd like to see Mr. Bigweld," Rodney said, trying to sound professional. "I'm an inventor."

"Oh." Tim nodded. "Why didn't you say so? Stand back."

Rodney did as he was told. He watched with excitement as Tim turned a large key in the lock and the gates magically swung open. "Thanks!" Rodney said, as he took his suitcase and began to walk through the gate.

Slam! Before Rodney could set foot behind the gated area, the giant doors crashed closed in front of him. "What?" he murmured, confused.

"Gotcha!" Tim laughed. He was greatly amused. "Ya see, you were all excited, and then boom!" He looked at Rodney's sad, surprised face. "All right, I had my laugh. Go in."

Once again, the gate opened majestically, allowing Rodney a full view of the buildings that housed Bigweld Industries. He stepped forward and . . .

Bam! The gate crashed closed right in front of him again. "Whoa, hey!" Rodney shouted angrily.

Tim was really having a good time now. "That's funny. The second time," the guard guffawed. "'Cause then you really think I'm gonna let you in. But I'm not."

Rodney wasn't laughing. "All right!" he shouted, fighting hard not to completely lose it. "We've all had a laugh—except me. Now let me in."

Tim shook his head. "Sorry, kid. Nobody gets in. Company rules."

"Company rules?" Rodney repeated. "Then how do they hire new inventors?"

"They don't. Those days are over." Tim stared thoughtfully at

Rodney. "My advice? Come back two years ago. Then the job is yours." He burst into a new round of hysterics. In fact, he laughed so hard, he shook an overhead balcony loose. It came down over his head. "Look what you made me do!" he shouted angrily at Rodney. "After I almost let you in . . . twice!"

Rodney had no pity for the wisecracking guard. He did, however, have a final warning for him. "I'll be back!" he vowed as he stalked away. "You can't stop me."

"Sure, I can!" Tim shouted back. "In fact, those are my orders. 'Keep out the losers!'"

"I'm not a loser!" Rodney insisted.

"No? Well, if you were a winner, you'd be up there with the big shots," Tim reminded him, as he pointed to the top of the high tower.

"You're right," Rodney said through clenched teeth. "And that's where I'm going. Up there!"

CHAPTER FIVE

Unfortunately, at the moment, Rodney wasn't up at all. He was way down—down in the streets and down on his luck. In fact, he was exactly the opposite of the successful, enterprising bot he had hoped to be.

Of the bots who'd made their way to the top, one sat higher than them all. The robot in the highest of those towers was Phineas T. Ratchet, the chief executive officer at Bigweld Industries. He was a state-of-the-art, fully upgraded bot, made of the finest steel. His body was an expensive gray-and-white pinstripe metal design, set off by a fiery red tie. He was the ultimate model of a corporate executive, the one the others measured themselves against.

At the very moment that Rodney was arguing with Tim, Ratchet was sitting at the head of a large conference table, watching an old episode of The Bigweld Show on a TV screen.

"You can shine no matter what you're made of," the image of Bigweld said.

Ratchet clicked the pause button on the TV and froze the image of the company's founder. "What a remarkable legacy. Concern for the common robot. Making life better! You don't hear that anymore. And for good reason . . ." He stopped and stared menacingly at the group of corporate executives who had gathered in the conference room. "There's no money in it!"

The executives nodded quietly.

"Memo to Bigweld," Ratchet continued, "we're not a charity! That's why old fatface no longer sits in the big chair. That's why I did all of us a favor and shoved, uh, ahem, er, I mean, showed him to the door. So I don't want to hear another 'Where's Bigweld? Where's Bigweld?' from any of you."

"We'll see him next month at the Bigweld Ball," one particularly dense executive said. "He always goes to that."

Ratchet glared at the bot. With a single push of a button, the executive and his chair fell through a hole in the floor. Within seconds, a new model executive popped up to take his place.

"Now, let's get down to business," Ratchet continued without missing a beat. "What's our big-ticket item?"

His underlings stared blankly into his eyes.

"Upgrades, people," Ratchet explained, exasperated. "Upgrades. That's how we make the dough. Now, if we're telling robots that no matter what they're made of they're fine, how can we expect them to feel crummy enough about themselves to buy our upgrades and make themselves look better?" He looked around the room. "Am I right?"

"He's right," one executive bot replied quickly.

"He's always right," agreed another.

"He's never wrong," said a third.

Ratchet smiled at their unbridled approvals. He would, of course, have expected nothing less from the bots who worked for him. Not if they wanted to keep their jobs. "Therefore, I've come up with a new slogan," Ratchet continued. "'Why be you, when you can be new?'"

Ratchet looked around the room. His employees stared back at him blankly. "I gotta tell ya, I think it's brilliant," the head bot told his underlings. "But honestly I'd like to hear what you employees think about this."

One executive exclaimed, "It's wonderful."

"I love it," seconded another.

"Woo-hoo! Out of the ballpark, boss!" shouted an exec bot named Forge.

Ratchet smiled at his team. They all seemed so enthusiastic. Well, all except one. Cappy—an attractive female bot with big blue eyes; high, round cheeks; a long, swanlike neck; and a particularly well-constructed top-of-the-line metal body—hadn't uttered her praise yet.

"Cappy, you haven't said a word," Ratchet reminded her. "What do you think of my idea?"

"It . . . gave me chills," she said slowly.

"Thank you," Ratchet replied.

"But . . ." Cappy continued.

Ratchet was shocked. No one ever used that word with him. "But?!" he demanded.

There was a collective gasp as the executives rolled their chairs as far away from Cappy as possible. No one wanted to be associated with someone who said "but" to Ratchet.

"Why would robots buy new upgrades if spare parts are so much cheaper?" Cappy continued, standing her ground.

"Oh, right. Well, that's easy, because as of today we are no longer making spare parts." As he spoke, Ratchet swept a box of spare parts from the table. They fell to the ground with a huge clatter.

Just in case that didn't make the executives spring to attention, Ratchet raised the volume of his mechanical voice a notch. "Do you know what I call outmodes? Scrap metal." Ratchet let out a haughty, hollow laugh and looked out the window at the regular robots down below. "You see them on the streets. Misshapen. Rust-covered." He shivered slightly with disgust. "They turn your insides out. You just want to go home and scrub yourself. And scrub and scrub and scrub and scrub and scrub and scrub and scrub . . ."

Seeing that the executives were slightly frightened by this sudden obsession with cleanliness, Ratchet forced himself to stop. He cleared his throat and tried to change the subject. "Has everyone seen Larry's new ride?" he asked nervously. "It's a honey."

Cappy wasn't paying attention to Ratchet any longer. She was busy looking out the window. Much to her surprise, a strange bot with a blue head and old hand-me-down replacement parts was holding onto a strange contraption made of an old teapot and spools and spoons that whirred like helicopter blades. He was flying in midair, right outside the conference room window. Of course, Cappy didn't know Rodney, or his Wonderbot, but she did know that whoever this robot was, he could only be one of two things: an absolute genius or a total nut. She was fascinated by him.

"Cappy," Ratchet purred, as he stepped closer to her. "I want your department to push our new slogan." He flashed her a smile, making sure she caught a glimpse of his recently shined teeth. "We'll be working very, very closely together on this one. Won't that be fun?"

Ratchet was so interested in Cappy's reaction to his latest statement that he didn't even hear the thud coming from the glass ceiling above the conference room as Rodney smacked into the glass.

"Oodles," Cappy told her boss. Her usually confident voice was tinged with discomfort at the idea of working so closely with Ratchet.

Before Ratchet could continue, there was a loud boom. Rodney and his Wonderbot tumbled through a skylight window in the glass ceiling and landed right on the conference room table.

Whoosh! Rodney slid along the length of the table, scattering paper, cups, eyeglasses, paper, and pens. He landed right on Cappy's lap. It only took a single instant—one quick glance into her big eyes—for Rodney to be smitten. He opened his mouth, eager to make a great first impression. "Uh . . . blah . . . bluh . . ." he babbled helplessly.

Cappy just stared at him.

The Wonderbot was shocked and more than a little scared by this latest fiasco. It darted across the room like a scared bird, zooming over the heads of some of the executive bots and heading straight for Ratchet. Rodney leaped up and dove for the Wonderbot just in time.

"Oh . . . so, sorry . . ." Rodney stammered, as he stroked and calmed his invention. "I—I . . ."

"What the—" Ratchet boomed.

The sound of his voice was very intimidating, but Rodney stood his ground. This was his chance, and he was taking it. "Sir, I—I . . . am a young inventor. It's always been my dream to come to Robot City and to present myself and my ideas to Mr.

Bigweld"—he looked around the room, anxiously searching for that familiar jolly face—"who doesn't seem to be here."

Ratchet cleared his throat and looked from Rodney to the Wonderbot and back. "Gee, no, but while he's away he left me in charge." Rodney's eyes grew wide with anticipation. This big, important executive was staring at his Wonderbot with great interest. "Oh, well, then. Let me show you what it can do."

"I have a better idea," Ratchet said. "Why don't you let me show you what it can do." He reached out and brutally grabbed the Wonderbot. "It can do this!" And he kicked the small invention right out the window!

"Aaaaahhhhh!" cried the Wonderbot.

"No!" Cappy gasped.

"Why you . . . I—I—" Rodney was so angry, he couldn't get the words out.

But Ratchet was never at a loss for words. He laughed in Rodney's face. "I—I . . ." he imitated Rodney's stammer. "Easy, killer. You're right. I was way out of line. To make it up to you, I'll show you around the place. . . ."

The next thing Rodney knew, he was hanging from a security

crane, dangling hundreds of stories above the street. A magnet was the only thing holding him to the crane's metal arm. Rodney looked down and shuddered. The bots below looked like tiny metal insects. If the crane let him go . . .

Crash! At that moment, the crane did exactly that! Rodney soared in the air for a moment. Then, smash! clammer! bash! He found himself lying in a heap on the sidewalk outside the gates of Bigweld Industries. Right back to where he'd started.

Things had already changed outside the gate. Construction bots had removed the sign that read YOU CAN SHINE NO MATTER WHAT YOU'RE MADE OF. They were tacking up a billboard that announced Bigweld Industries' new slogan: WHY BE YOU, WHEN YOU CAN BE NEW?

Rodney groaned and sat up. The magnetic pull had attracted a lot of thin metal filings to his face. He attempted to wipe them away, but he was still magnetized and the filings just wouldn't fall. Rodney pushed the slivers of black metal from his cheeks, and they leaped into formation under his nose. He tried to wipe away the metal moustache, and the filings moved to his cheeks and chin, giving him a thick pair of sideburns and a beard. Another swipe from Rodney's hand and the filings moved up to his forehead, giving him big bushy eyebrows and a wacky hair-do.

"So, how'd it go?" Tim the guard asked sarcastically, as he spotted Rodney playing with his face.

Rodney stood up and glared at the snide guard. "What the heck's going on around here?" he demanded. "Some highly polished jerk is sitting in Bigweld's chair!"

"And you're sitting on the sidewalk," Tim reminded him.

Rodney grimaced. "You know, someday you'll be working for me!" he told Tim.

Rodney's determination set Tim off on a new round of guffaws. "Oh, really?" he giggled hysterically. "Can I have Tuesdays off?"

Rodney didn't answer. Instead, he stood, turned, and walked down the street. Even his Wonderbot was gone now. Rodney was truly alone in Robot City. And he just couldn't shake the electromagnetic power that had held him to the crane. For the first time in his life, Rodney had what you could call a magnetic personality. Unfortunately, what he was currently attracting were garbage cans, a Dumpster, a few spare bot parts, and other random pieces of metal he passed by.

A garbage pail lid attached itself to Rodney's back.

Immediately, the quick-thinking bot pulled it off and began to use it as a shield to protect himself from the seemingly endless stream of oncoming metal debris.

But the shield was not enough to protect Rodney from an oxygen tank that fell from a nearby wall and tripped Rodney. He flipped over and sparks flew off his body, igniting the gas in the oxygen tank. Boom! Rodney rocketed down the street.

Crash! As a rocket, Rodney zoomed right into the huge billboard that read WELCOME TO ROBOT CITY. The flying junk behind him pushed him straight through the billboard, and he landed on the other side inside a battered trash can.

CHAPTER SIX

Rodney had no idea how long he'd been inside the trash can, but when he finally came to, he could hear someone singing outside.

"I'm a little teapot, short and stout," the bot sang in a high, squeaky voice. "Here is my handle, here is my spout. When I get all steamed up, hear me shout, just tip me over and pour me out!"

As he gathered himself, Rodney felt a strange twisting sensation in his leg. Had he sprained his ankle? Dented a toe? No. That wasn't it. Then, suddenly, it hit him. This little teapot was unscrewing Rodney's foot!

"Hey!" Rodney shouted angrily.

It was Fender, the odd, gangly bot who had been on the Crosstown Express with Rodney.

"Oh, hi there. Uh, listen, if I seem to be getting smaller, it's because I'm leaving! Foot don't fail me now!"

"Stop! Hey! You've got my foot!" Rodney called after him, as the weird bot ran away. Rodney struggled to stand, but he was stuck in the trash can. He was forced to go after the bot with the can on his back, like a turtle inside its shell.

The rusty red bot was fast, but not all that careful. He ran right into a rickety tower of old tin cans stacked high in the air. As he leaped out of the way of the cans, he crashed into Rodney. The sheer force of the collision knocked the trash can from Rodney's back. Luckily, he was no longer magnetized.

Fender darted nervously down a narrow alleyway. Rodney limped after him. Then, things suddenly went from bad to worse. One of the cans filled with round ball bearings came crashing down. Before Rodney knew what was happening, a sea of slippery metal balls flooded the alley.

The torrent of oncoming ball bearings surprised Fender. He stopped for a second, giving Rodney the chance he needed to grab hold of his own toes on the foot Fender was holding. But Fender wasn't giving up so easily. He held on tight to the heel of the metal foot. Before either of them knew what was happening, they were in a foot-tug-of-war!

The two robots slipped and slid over the metal balls. They looked like a pair of ice-dancing bots. But this was no dance. For Rodney, this was a matter of survival. For Fender, it was a simple case of finder's keepers. Neither one of them was going to give up easily.

Fender yanked harder on his end of the stolen foot. The sheer force sent him flying out of control into a pile of tin cans. He landed with a crash. Boing! His head popped off.

"Ow!" the bodyless head moaned at Rodney. "Happy now?"

"Not till you give me back my foot, you mugger!" Rodney yanked his missing body part back.

"I am not a mugger!" Fender's head insisted. "I happen to be a scrounger. I didn't know you were at the end of that foot."

Rodney sat on the ground and focused his attention on reattaching his foot to the bottom of his leg. When he was finished, he turned back to the headless robot. "Oh, here," he said, reaching for the skull. "Let me help you with that."

Fender's head shook itself. "No, no, no," it declared. "I'll do it myself. I have my pride you know." It let out a sharp whistle, and its body ran over to it. The body reached out its arms, but because it had no eyes, it couldn't be sure where the head might be.

"Over here. Oh, no, not that close," the head moaned, as Fender's foot accidentally kicked it over. "Oh, hold on. Hold on . . ." Fender's body moved a little to the right and managed to kick its head once again. "Ow! No, no, no. Ow! Aaah!" the head shouted painfully, as Fender's foot kicked it like a football. Fender's poor head bounced down through a series of discarded lead pipes, and landed in a shopping cart piled high with scrap metal. "Oooh. Unk. Oonk. . . ." The head moaned.

At that moment, a gang of odd-looking bots entered the alleyway. The Rusties, as they were known, were scrounging for odd parts and scraps. When they heard Fender's head scream, they came running over.

Lug, a big, chubby green bot, was the first to spot the rolling head. "Hey, Fender, how's it going?" he greeted him.

"'How's it going?'" a thin, grumpy robot named Crank Casey repeated, as if he couldn't believe Lug would ask such a question. Crank twisted his tubelike neck so he could get a better look at the state Fender was in. "What? He's a head in a basket! We're doomed," he moaned. "I knew it. We're doomed."

"Will you shut up, you neurotic nut?" Fender's head scolded. "Why, I'd . . . I'd smack you if I had a hand!" The head looked up. "Whoa!" Fender shouted. "Speak of the devil, here I come!" At that moment, Fender's headless body landed right on top of his bodyless head. "Oww!"

Rodney watched as the run-down robots came to the aid of their friend's head and body. Then, suddenly, a perky girl bot with pigtails popped out of the Dumpster. She was holding the Wonderbot!

"Hey, check this out," the teenage bot, named Piper Pinwheeler, told her friends. "Who would throw away such a cute little doodad?" Then she noticed Fender's head in the shopping cart. "Fender?" she asked. "What happened to you?"

Rodney couldn't believe his good fortune. That bot had found his invention! "Hey, that's mine!" he insisted.

"That's him!" Fender's head cried out. His arm pointed straight ahead at nothing. "That's the guy! I would know that face. I know that face and I know that foot."

"I'm over here," Rodney called out.

Fender's arm pointed in the direction of Rodney's voice. "That's the perpetrator. He knocked my head off." The body poised itself for a fight. "You want another piece of me?"

That was all Piper needed to hear. She leaped from the Dumpster and raced over to Rodney. "All right, Buster! If you think you can mess with my big brother, you . . . you're kind of cute." She eyed Rodney curiously as Lug tried to reattach Fender's head to his body. Unfortunately, he jammed the head on upside down.

Crank rolled his eyes at Piper's flirtation. "Piper, would you behave yourself?" he scolded her. "Now, let's get Fender fixed . . . again."

Piper handed Rodney the Wonderbot. "Here's your thingamabob," she said, as she began to walk off with her friends. "See ya around."

Two of Fender's friends led his body away from the alleyway, and a third carried his head. Even though he'd lost his head, Fender hadn't lost his mind . . . or his tongue. He had plenty to say to his little sister. "I've told you a hundred times," he scolded her. "Don't talk to strange men!"

Piper frowned. "I talk to you," she muttered to herself. "Who's stranger than that?"

*

The Rusties carried Fender to Jack Hammer's Hardware Store. Jack, the owner of the shop, almost always had the parts Fender needed. Today, though, it was a different story.

Jack had good news and bad news for Fender.

"What's the bad news?" Fender asked him nervously.

"I checked the stock book, and as of today, they are no longer making parts for your model," Jack said, breaking the news as gently as he could. "You have been officially outmoded."

"Outmoded, that's just fine." Fender groaned. "What's the good news?"

"Well," Jack replied, "when we had your parts, they were on sale. Ha, ha, ha."

Fender didn't see the humor at all. Outmoded! It was enough to make a grown bot cry. "How could this happen to me? I'm practically a kid!"

"Gee, look, pull yourself together," Jack urged him, suddenly feeling sorry for having joked around. "All you need is an upgrade." He hurried into the back and came out with a carton of fresh parts.

"Whoa!" the Rusties exclaimed in unison as Jack set a part onto the counter.

"Mmm . . ." Lug sniffed at the air. "That new upgrade smell."

"Just came in, fully loaded," Jack informed them. "Look, it's got cup holders, standard!"

Lug's eyes grew large with excitement. "Does it come in plus sizes?"

"Sure!" Jack told the big, green Rusty. "Take a look at Bigweld's new spring collection." He pointed to a vast selection of replacement parts in various shapes and sizes.

The Rusties loved the look of the new models. Fender, however, was far less impressed. "I can't afford that fancy stuff," he reminded the others. "All I need is one stinking neck joint!" Fender's head began banging itself on the counter. "Why . . . did . . . this . . . happen . . . to . . . me?" the head moaned as it banged again and again. Then it frowned. "I'm hurting me. Idiot!"

Rodney entered the store just in time to hear the shopkeeper tell Fender the worst news of all.

"Sorry, pal," Jack informed him. "It's either an upgrade or the Chop Shop for you."

Fender's head gulped. "The Chop Shop?" He began to panic. "No, look at me! I have a warranty, don't I? Come on!

Somebody, there has to be a warranty somewhere on me." He frantically looked to his friends for help. They stared back at him blankly.

"I'm fine. I'm fine. I'm fine." Fender tried to assure everyone. He began to juggle his head. "Hey, hey, hey. Hup, hup, hup. Oh." He propped his head precariously on top of his neck. "Ta-da! I'm back!" he announced, as though he were finishing some sort of psycho magic trick. "Miss me?"

That got Piper's attention. "No one's going to the Chop Shop." She stared menacingly into Jack's eyes and grabbed him by the throat. "Listen, shiny pants," she warned. "You get back there and find a part for my brother. We are not junk. We are not scrap. And we will not be treated this way!"

But there was nothing Jack could do. "I'm sorry," he told her. "I don't have the parts."

"Well, do you have two washers, an S-spring, and some fast weld?" Rodney interrupted.

The Rusties all turned to look at him.

Rodney smiled at Fender's head. "I can fix you easily," he assured him. It was true. After years of working on the Wonderbot, Rodney had become an expert at putting things together on a low budget. Compared to the Wonderbot, connecting Fender's head was a simple job, despite the fact that his body wasn't exactly in tip-top shape.

"When was the last time you got oiled?" Rodney asked Fender a few moments later, as he sat on the side of a busy street, reattaching the bot's rusty red head to his neck.

"I can't really answer that with my kid sister around," Fender confided.

"Can it, Fender!" Piper barked. She was tired of being treated like a child.

Rodney rotated Fender's head to the left. "Hold still," he warned. "This might tickle."

He wasn't kidding. Fender giggled uncontrollably as Rodney moved his head back and forth. When the work was finished, the outmoded Rusty looked up at the young inventor and smiled. "We haven't been properly introduced. I'm Fender. Used to be Bumper, but I had to change it when we came into the country."

"Copperbottom," Rodney introduced himself. "Rodney Copperbottom."

"Copperbottom," Fender repeated in a snooty voice. "Oh, hey, everyone! Rodney's here. The Rodster. Hello, Rod. If I'd known you were coming, I'd have cleaned myself up." Fender stopped talking long enough to ask a question that had been bothering him. "Hey, riddle me this: Why did I meet you among the garbage?"

Rodney thought back on his "meeting" at Bigweld Industries and sighed. "It's a long story."

Fender shrugged. "In that case, skip it."

Piper slapped Fender on the crank, and then sidled up next to Rodney. "I want to hear," she assured him.

"Well, today I tried to get in to see Bigweld," Rodney began, encouraged by her interest in his tale.

"Hey, lots of luck," Piper interrupted him. "Bigweld's gone. It's like there never was a Bigweld."

Rodney couldn't . . . wouldn't . . . believe it. "Of course there's a Bigweld."

Piper shot him a skeptical look. "Well, if you find him, tell him we really need him to come back. He cared about bots like us."

"What I heard is that they did him in and they left the rest of us to fall apart. That's why there's no part for Fender's neck. Diesel needs a new voice box, too."

As if to prove it, Diesel Springer opened his mouth wide. A

ball flew out, but not a sound emerged.

"And when you totally fall apart, you become sweeper bait," Fender added as the ball raced off.

"You mean . . . ?" Rodney gasped.

At that very moment, a sweeper rode by, looking for an unsuspecting outmoded bot to eat. It swallowed up the ball in a single bite.

Fender pointed the sweeper out to Rodney. "Straight to the Chop Shop."

But right now, thanks to Rodney's skills, Fender would be avoiding that fate. His head was perfectly attached. In fact, he could spin it around and around—and he hadn't been able to do that for years. "Hey, look at that! He fixed my neck!" he cheered as it circled around.

But Rodney didn't feel like celebrating his success. He was too upset about the disappearance of Bigweld. He needed to go someplace where he could think things through. "I guess I'd better get going," Rodney told the Rusties.

"Where you heading?" Piper asked.

"Well, I've given it a lot of thought . . . and I have no idea," Rodney admitted.

Suddenly, Fender whipped out an imaginary microphone and, for no apparent reason, took on the role of a crazed game show announcer. "When in Robot City, guests of the Rusties—that's us—stay at Aunt Fan's Boarding House, where our motto is, 'Beats rustin' outside.'"

Rodney looked at him gratefully. "You sure?"

Fender, Piper, and the rest of the Rusties all rushed to assure him that he was welcome.

As they watched the sweeper ride off to the Chop Shop, Fender leaped into the street and wiggled his butt. "Here's one outmode you're not gonna get!" he taunted. "Na-na-na-na-na! Na-na-na-na-na!"

Clank! His butt slipped right off its hinge and landed at his ankles. "Whoops," Fender added, blushing even redder than usual.

As Fender and his pals led Rodney through the streets of Robot City to Aunt Fan's Boarding House, they had no idea that some truly dastardly deeds were going on underground . . . at the Chop Shop.

Madame Gasket, a frighteningly grotesque bot, was hard at work, ordering her minions to do her evil bidding. "All right, break time!" she called out to them. A second later, she said, "All right, break time over!" Her workers were amazed. That had been a much longer break than usual!

Such was life for the bots who worked the maze of conveyor belts at the Chop Shop, sorting out the pieces of outmoded bots who had long since passed their prime. There was no relaxation for them. Madame Gasket saw to that. She laughed haughtily, stopping only when a visitor arrived in the shop.

"Well, look who's here," she said with mock respect.

"Hi, Mom," Ratchet replied.

"How's my boy?"

Ratchet smiled proudly. "Great. I did what you told me. No more spare parts. In a couple of weeks all those broken-down losers out there will be nothing but scrap metal. You will be up to your bloomers in outmoded junk."

"Such a good boy," Madame Gasket praised her son. "And after you finish off Bigweld, there will be nobody out there to fix them."

"Exactly!" Ratchet cheered. Then he paused for a moment. He had absolutely no idea what his mother was talking about. "Um, you want to run that by me again?"

"You heard me. I want you to destroy Bigweld."

Ratchet gasped. That was more than he'd bargained for. "That wasn't part of the plan. He's not going to be any trouble where he is. He—"

Madame Gasket was exasperated. "What are you afraid of? This is what's always held you back. Be strong! Show some bolts! Or do you want to end up like you father?"

She grabbed her son by the collar and held him high above the ground so he could get a better view of his dad, who was dangling pathetically from a high wire, his joints squeaking in the breeze. Ratchet gulped. His mother was capable of some pretty awful things.

"With Bigweld gone, all our dreams will come true," she cooed deviously, cradling Ratchet's head in her arms.

"Okay, Mommy," Ratchet said finally, not wanting to disappoint her. "Destroy Bigweld. I'm putting it on my to-do list."

Madame Gasket smiled at her child, quite pleased. "Are you hungry?" she asked him. "Can I get you something? You look thin."

"No, Mom, I gotta go," Ratchet replied, as he hurried out of the Chop Shop. He stopped and turned to the pathetic robot hanging from the ceiling. "Bye, Pop.'"

"So long, son," Mr. Gasket squawked in his meek voice. "Good luck with your dastardly plans."

CHAPTER SEVEN

Fender and the other Rusties had no idea that Ratchet and his mother were planning to remove all the outmoded bots in Robot City from the streets. At the moment, thoughts of the Chop Shop were far from their minds, because they were welcoming Rodney into their home for the night.

Fender opened the door to Aunt Fan's home and led Rodney inside. The boarding house certainly wasn't like the neat, orderly house Rodney had grown up in. In the Copperbottom home, everything was simple, with basic furniture and no clutter. But here . . . well, it was amazing. The living room was filled with unusual sculptures, overstuffed couches, and other strange objects Aunt Fan had collected over the years. It was cluttered and cozy.

"Let me just let her know you're here," Fender said, as Rodney studied the unusual decor. "Aunt Fan!" he shouted. "We brought someone!"

"I'm in the kitchen!" Aunt Fan sang back joyfully.

"Are you sure your aunt won't mind?" Rodney asked Fender nervously.

"Relax. She's not my aunt. She just takes in bots who are, um, broke. Bless her little heart," Fender added sincerely, as he directed Rodney into the kitchen of the boarding house.

"Then why do you call her Aunt Fan?" Rodney wondered.

"We couldn't call her Aunt Booty," Fender replied.

Not that that wouldn't have been appropriate in her case. After all, Aunt Fan wasn't just any bot. She was a unique combination of parts with a brightly painted cheerful face, a metallic hairdo piled high on her head like a beehive, and multicolored crystals that decorated her torso. But her most unique feature was her massive rear end. It was huge, with round dials and shiny bits of metal that made it stand out even more, if that were possible. She was obviously very proud of her incredible derriere.

"Whoa!" Rodney exclaimed with obvious amazement as he caught sight of the woman. The word was out of his mouth before he could stop himself. He could feel the grease rising to his cheeks with embarrassment.

But Rodney needn't have worried. Aunt Fan didn't hear him. The sound of Rodney's voice was masked by the clatter of pots and pans falling from the counter. Aunt Fan had knocked them over as she turned to greet Fender and his friend. Apparently, Aunt Fan had little control over her huge caboose.

"Whoops! Oh, scrap," she exclaimed, as she tried to leap out of the way of a falling frying pan. Too late. It landed on her toe. "Oh, owww," she moaned. "Right on my shoes. I'm so clumsy." The landlady sighed and smiled at Rodney. "Well, hello there. What's your name?"

Rodney tried to focus on Aunt Fan's face, but he just couldn't move his eyes from her enormous tush. "I'm Rodney Bigbottom," he blurted out. "No, um, I'm Rodney Copperbottom. Copperbottom."

"That's a wonderful name," Aunt Fan complimented him sincerely. "Bigbottom."

As Aunt Fan turned to speak to Fender, a horn started to beep. It sounded like a truck backing up in the street. Rodney didn't recognize the noise at first, but he'd never forget it. It was Aunt Fan's fanny signal. She was backing up. Before he could leap out of the way, Aunt Fan backed into Rodney, smothering his entire body with her rear end and pinning him to the wall.

"Well, I . . ." she began to say to Fender. Then she noticed Rodney had disappeared. "What happened to your friend?" She quickly turned her body to look for the missing bot.

"Whoa!" Rodney cried out once again, as Aunt Fan's fanny shifted position and freed him. He gasped for air.

Aunt Fan giggled. "Oh, there you are."

"Aunt Fan, he needs a place to stay," Fender explained.

"Well, just make yourself at home," she told Rodney sincerely.

"Thank you. That's very kind of you," he replied.

"My pleasure," she said sincerely. "See a need, fill a need."

"Hey, just like Bigweld," Rodney recalled.

The thought of Bigweld struck a chord in Aunt Fan. She found him downright handsome. "Ooh, Bigweld," she gushed. "That's a lot of robot!" She turned around suddenly, and her butt knocked Rodney and Fender all the way into the living room. They landed with a thud on the couch.

"Come on, you can bunk with me," Fender invited Rodney. He

walked across the room and pulled on a giant lever. Suddenly, that entire side of the room began to rotate on its side like a giant Ferris wheel. As the wheel turned, each of the rooms in the boarding house came into view.

Rodney watched in amazement as one by one the Rusties' bedrooms passed in front of him. He could see Piper in her room. She was wrapped in a metallic towel, and her face was covered in wax. She was obviously not expecting company. She gasped when she saw the boys.

"Fender, get out of my room!" she demanded.

"I'm not in your room," Fender argued. Then, he moved one foot across the threshold. "I am now," he teased. Then, moving his foot out again, he said, "No, I'm not."

Piper wasn't in the mood for games. She held the wax buffer menacingly in his direction. "Get outta my room!" she repeated.

"Moving on," Fender told Rodney, as he pulled the lever, sending the wheel moving again. Suddenly, Rodney found himself face-to-face with Crank Casey. The rusting bot was squatting over a pan, reading a newspaper. They'd caught him going to the bathroom!

"Oh, man, this is my third oil change today. Something's wrong with me," Crank informed them.

"Oops, sorry," Fender apologized, as he pulled the lever one more time and revealed his own room. Rodney stared at his new home away from home. It was a complete pigsty. A total mess!

"Here we are, home sweet home," Fender announced grandly. "What's mine is yours." He flung out his arms excitedly . . . and they fell off. "Oh, dear."

"I'll get them," Rodney reassured him.

But that wasn't so easy. Fender's arms were already busy on their own. "Look at that, they're arm wrestling. Could you separate them?" he asked Rodney. The gangly red robot grimaced and scratched his back against the wall. "Hurry. My backside itches!"

Rodney had never had a roommate before. He'd never had the chance to enjoy stimulating late-night guy talk, like the kind Fender was offering him that evening. Right now, weird squeaks were coming from Fender's side of the room.

Fender looked over at Rodney's disgusted expression and shook his head. "I'm doing musical arm farts. Do you know how to do those? They're hard to do, because we're made of metal. But that's where the skill comes in. Listen." He placed his hand under his armpit and squeezed. A loud squeak emerged. Fender smiled proudly.

Rodney shook his head. "You know, I'm a little tired," he replied. "Maybe tomorrow."

Fender studied Rodney's weary steel face. "Kind of a rough day, huh?"

"Kinda," Rodney admitted. "My dad's probably sitting by the phone waiting for his brilliant son to call and tell him what a big success his first day was." Rodney stopped himself mid-sentence and took a deep breath. "It's not your problem. If you burden your friends, soon you won't have any."

"What are you? A fortune cookie?" Fender joked. Then he considered what Rodney had just said. "You consider me a friend?"

"Sure. What else would I consider you?"

"I don't know." Fender shrugged. "An embarrassment, a way to rebel against your parents, a desperate cry for help? The list is endless."

Rodney smiled slightly. "Let's just stick with friend."

Fender nodded understandingly. "Well, Rodney, even though you had a discouraging day, remember, there's another one coming tomorrow."

Rodney was quiet for a moment, thinking. Then he said, "Hey, Fender."

"Hmm?"

Rodney placed his hand under his armpit and let out a string of the loudest arm farts ever.

Fender collapsed into a fit of giggles. "Catchy tune." He began to sing, "Let your hand go. Let it now, let it now, make those sounds below. Let that little air bumpin'. Let it start a pumpin'."

Soon, the entire house was in on the fun. Although the party started to wind down after Aunt Fan didn't quite get the arm part of arm farts.

CHAPTER EIGHT

Morning seemed to come quickly. Before Rodney knew what was happening, the lampposts had turned themselves off and wearily headed for home. The sun was up, and Aunt Fan was busy in the kitchen cooking breakfast for her boarders.

The Rusties clinked and clanked their way to the table. They seemed to be lost in an early morning wake-up fog. But Aunt Fan had just the remedy: a cup of freshly brewed grease.

"Mmm," the Rusties moaned as they slathered the oil all over their bodies. They began to perk up. Nothing wakes up a bot quite like a cup of hot oil in the morning.

"So what are you guys going to do today?"

"We're doing it," Fender said.

"Bigweld's disappeared and you're just sitting here?" Rodney was incredulous.

"I think that's already been established," Fender replied.

Rodney couldn't believe it. "The idol of millions is gone missing, and we're just kickin' back?"

Fender gave him a curious look. "Are you going somewhere with this?"

"It's wrong!" Rodney admonished him. "Isn't anyone programmed for outrage anymore? There should be rioting in the streets!"

"Aaaaahhhhhhhhhhhhh!" No sooner had the words left Rodney's mouth when a mob of robots came charging down the street, screaming at the top of their lungs.

"Hey, that was great," Fender told Rodney. "Now say, 'Money should be falling from the sky.'"

Rodney could barely hear him as the screaming bots raced by. He and the Rusties ran out of the boarding house and followed them. As it turned out, every bot in the crowd was heading to Jack Hammer's Hardware Store. They had only one thing on their minds.

"Parts! Parts!" the rioting bots cried out. "We want parts!"

Jack stood outside his store, addressing the angry crowd. "Sorry, folks. All sold out," he told them. "Nothing but upgrades from now on."

The crowd watched as gleaming new upgrades were unloaded from a truck and brought into the store. The sign on the side of the truck read, WHY BE YOU, WHEN YOU CAN BE NEW?"

"I like myself the way I am!" a lightbulb bot declared with such vehemence that her bulb burst.

"We don't want upgrades!" a bolt bot agreed.

One furious bot had had enough. He picked up a trash can and aimed it at the storefront window. "Let's get him!" he cried out.

But the trash can wasn't having any of that. "What are you doing? Don't throw me!" he shouted. Then the can spotted Rodney coming around the corner. "Hey, look!" he cried out, pointing in Rodney's direction. "Isn't that the guy who fixed Fender's neck?"

A buzz went through the crowd. Somehow, they'd all heard the story of Rodney's great deed.

"That guy fixes bots!" one of the rioters shouted out excitedly.

"Yeah! That kid can help you," Jack said, happily turning the attention from himself.

"Brace yourself," Fender whispered to Rodney. "You're about to get very popular."

In an instant the mob turned their attention to Rodney. They raced toward him.

The first bot to reach Rodney looked up at him with pleading eyes. "Parts, man! I need parts!"

Rodney reached out and touched him gently. "You don't look that bad," he began, just before the outmoded bot fell to pieces.

A nearby bot leaped at the opportunity. "Hey, everybody! Spare parts!" he said, grabbing for pieces of the broken bot.

And he wasn't the only one. In their desperation, the rioting bots began to pick away at the metal carcass on the ground. Rodney tried to stop them. "What's wrong with you robots?" he demanded. "You have to stick together! Take care of one another!"

Fender stood tall and backed him up. "That's right," he added. "You should all be ashamed of yourselves." It was a powerful statement, which would have been a lot more convincing had Fender not been wearing two noses at the time.

Fender sheepishly removed the extra nose he'd swiped from the broken-down outmoded bot. "Sorry," he apologized. "I just got caught up."

An outmoded bot named Smelt walked up to Rodney and held out his hand. "Hey, could you look at my arm?" he asked.

Rodney shook the bot's hand—and it fell off.

"Uh, nice grip," Rodney told him.

"Like iron," Smelt replied proudly.

Another outmoded bot handed Rodney a well-worn rear end. "I haven't sat down in weeks," he said, asking for a repair.

Yet another bot held out a pair of metal eyeballs. "My eyes fell out!"

"I can't get rid of this spare tire," a chubby bot said, placing his hands around his rubber-treaded midsection.

"I'm losing my mind!" cried another bot.

The crowd surged in, with hundreds of bots screaming out their requests.

"See a need, fill a need," Rodney murmured quietly.

*

That day was just the beginning. Rodney and the Rusties created an entire clinic designed to help the outmoded and forgotten bots of the world. The clinic worked like a well-oiled machine in which each bot played a part. Aunt Fan took temperatures. Fender assisted in the examining room. Lug used his brute strength to prepare patients by unscrewing their heads for examination. Piper welded rusted metal with a blowtorch, and Diesel painted faces on faceless bots. (Of course from time to time he painted them on the backs of their heads, but hey, at least they had faces!) The Wonderbot was a big help, too.

The Rusties also asked each bot if he or she had seen Bigweld. The Wonderbot even flew around showing a picture of the big man to all the broken-down bots in line. No one had seen him lately.

As it turned out, Rodney was quite an innovative doctor. He might not have had actual replacement parts to work with, but he was able to come up with all sorts of ways to fix broken bots. He replaced one bot's missing leg by bending the bot's crutch and attaching it where his leg would have been. That bot danced the whole way home! He gave Smelt an extendo-arm, then shook his hand before sending him on his way. He even used a plunger to unclog a toilet bot.

From then on, Rodney spent his days tightening heads, reattaching arms, fixing tickers, changing oil, and reprogramming innards. He went without sleeping, eating, or bathing for two straight weeks as he helped rebuild bots. But it all was worth it. This was his chance to make a difference.

Rodney's fame was growing. Outmoded bots of all shapes and sizes traveled daily from miles around to seek his help. And the broken-down bots weren't the only ones who knew of Rodney's innovative genius.

Word of his talents had even spread to the underground Chop Shop. Madame Gasket wasn't at all pleased. She hurried over to Bigweld Industries and burst into her son's office, unannounced. Ratchet was in the middle of a massage and had given strict orders not to be disturbed, but that didn't stop her. Madame Gasket had only one issue on her mind: The bot doc had to be stopped!

"Aagh?!" Ratchet screamed, as his mother suddenly

appeared in his office, standing beside his massage table. Ratchet was scared by her appearance. (Of course, she had that effect on a lot of people.)

Madame Gasket pointed to a fresh hole in the wall. "I came up the air shaft," she told her son. "I know you don't like anyone here to see me."

Ratchet wasn't surprised. His mother was capable of many things. Now that he knew how she'd gotten there, the big question on his mind was why. "What do you want?" he asked her.

"Someone's fixing them!" the evil bot told her son.

"What?"

Madame Gasket's eyes bulged. Steam popped out of her head. "Am I speaking in a foreign language?!" she exploded. "Someone is repairing outmodes and keeping them going. Keeping them on the streets. And they're laughing at you!"

"Whoa!" Ratchet stopped her. "Are you sure they're not laughing with me?"

"Yes."

"Oh, so what if one crazy fanatic repairs a few outmodes?" Ratchet asked. "Who cares?"

Madame Gasket rolled her eyes in disgust. "Think! Use those brains I stole for you! Today, it's one! What about tomorrow when everyone gets the idea that this is okay?" She was really upset now. "'We can fix ourselves!" she shouted, imitating the outmode population. "'We don't need upgrades!' Then what happens to you?"

Ratchet seemed frightened. He'd never seen his mother this mad, which was saying a lot. "Okay, okay, take it easy," he said, trying to calm her down before she did something to him. "We've got to find out who this bot is and stop him."

"Not stop him—crush him. Destroy him," Madame Gasket declared. And then you'll build me more sweepers and we'll take the rest of the outmodes off the streets—alive!" She stopped her tantrum long enough to reach into her bag and pull out a photo in a heart-shaped frame. "Oh, and by the way, I brought you a little something." She placed her gruesome image on her son's desk.

Ratchet stared at the cold, angry eyes in the photo. His mother would now be staring back at him from his desk every day.

Rodney worked his magic on hundreds of bots. Aunt Fan

generously donated her living room as a temporary hospital. They worked as a team, shocking an old bot's tickers into ticking and giving new voices to opera singers.

Finally, everyone slumped in Aunt Fan's living room for a much-needed break. Rodney felt like he had just been on a two-week, nonstop ride on the Crosstown Express. He dumped a cup of grease over himself and then tried to rally.

"Is there anyone else waiting?" He asked no one in particular.

Fender glanced out the window. "A few." He reported back.

Rodney went to see for himself. "A few?" There were hundreds of bots lined up down the street.

"What did you expect, Rodney?" Piper joined them at the window. "Bigweld was gone. They had nowhere to turn. But then came Copperbottom! I'm getting all staticky just thinking about it."

Rodney wasn't feeling staticky at all. In fact, he was feeling totally overwhelmed. "I'm not Bigweld. I don't have parts!"

Just then, Aunt Fan's local mailbox, Otis, barged in. "Mail call! Mail call!" He shouted. "Copperbottom, this one's from your mom."

Rodney would have liked a little more privacy to read his

letter, but he was anxious for the news from Rivet Town so he opened it right away.

"Is anything wrong?" Piper asked him. She had been watching his face as he read.

The extremely helpful mailbox decided to save Rodney the trouble of answering. "Yeah, his father's starting to clunk along. And, of course, those small-town junkheads can't find a new part for him. Don't worry. He's got a few thousand miles left in him."

Rodney was about to blow. "Did you read my mail?" He practically shouted at Otis.

But he shouldn't have worried about hurting the mailbox's feelings. "Obviously," said the cheeky bot before sauntering out to continue his rounds.

"Rodney, are you really worried about your Dad?" Piper asked, trying not to sound like she hoped the answer was no.

"Do you have to go home?" Aunt Fan chimed in, sounding even more anxious.

"If I go home, I still can't help him." Rodney pointed out calmly. "We're out of parts, we've got to get to Bigweld. He's the only one that can fix this."

He was interrupted by a tap on the window. The Wonderbot

was outside. He was bobbing around frantically like a little kid with something very, very important to say. Finally, he unrolled a poster: BIGWELD BALL TONIGHT, it read. Fender and Rodney exchanged glances.

"Of course! The Bigweld Ball. You can't have the Bigweld Ball without Bigweld," Aunt Fan exclaimed gleefully.

"Well, that's it, then," Rodney declared firmly. "I'm going to the Bigweld Ball."

"Oh, yeah," Crank snickered sarcastically. "You're right at the top of that guest list."

CHAPTER NINE

That evening, Rodney bravely returned to Bigweld Industries. He stood in front of the same gate and faced the same guard. But this time, he refused to end up on the wrong side of the gate. He was going to get to Bigweld. He had to. The lives of too many bots depended on it.

Bigweld hadn't been anywhere near his offices the last time Rodney had dropped in. But now he was certain that Bigweld was going to be present. After all, tonight was the big, fancy corporate party. Bigweld always attended that event. All Rodney had to do was find a way to crash the party. Once he was in, he'd make Bigweld listen to him.

Of course, getting into a private executive party at Bigweld Industries was easier said than done. Everyone had to pass through a security checkpoint where Tim the guard made sure only invited guests got past the red velvet rope. There was no chance that Rodney Copperbottom was one of the names on the guest list. But Rodney wasn't going to let that stop him. He had a secret weapon that was sure to help him gain admittance to the party. He had Fender!

Fender and Rodney waited nervously in line as the guests made their way through the security stop. Rodney was tense beneath his homemade bulky upgrades—a disguise he'd created to fool Tim and the executives who were sure to recognize him. He and Fender had rehearsed their plan over and over again.

When they were next in line to talk to Tim, Fender strutted over to the guard and adjusted the cape he'd thrown on as his costume. The disguised Rusty pointed to Rodney and proudly announced, "This is the Count Roderick von Brokenzipper, formerly known as Count Velcro."

Tim looked down, scanning his list for the name, but Fender immediately interrupted his train of thought. "Where are the trumpets?" he demanded, sounding very official.

"The what?" Tim asked. He seemed confused.

"We were promised trumpets to announce the Count's arrival," Fender continued. He turned to Rodney and lowered his head in shame. "I am sorry, your grace. Beat me until you're happy."

Rodney reached out his hand and pretended to slap Fender. Of course, he was careful not to make contact with his friend's body. There was no telling when an old part might pop off and spoil their disguises.

"He's happy," Fender reported to Tim. He began to lead Rodney into the party.

"You're not on the list," Tim said, barring them from taking another step.

A look of horror crossed Fender's face. "We're . . ." he began. Turning to Rodney he said, "Once again."

Rodney obediently pretended to slap Fender.

"Thank you," Fender replied. He turned and glared at Tim. "Fine! We will go!" he agreed angrily. "You will explain to your superiors why the Count was not able to attend their little luau, barn dance, or whatever this is. We are leaving in a huff!"

Tim had seen what happened to people who had to explain

their mistakes to Ratchet, and he had no desire to visit the trash compactor. He leaped to the side and cleared the way immediately. "No, no, please go in," he urged them. "In fact, would the Count like to hit me?"

Fender was aghast. "The Count? Hit you? The arrogance of some people. I will hit you." He reached up a metal fist and clobbered the guard. Tim fell off his guard platform. "Oh, thank you, your grace," he said.

As Rodney climbed over Tim's injured limbs, he whispered gratefully to his pal, "Fender, that was brilliant."

Fender removed his hat to bow and the Wonderbot flew out from under it.

"Okay, let's split up," Rodney suggested. "If you see Bigweld, come find me. If anything goes wrong, we'll signal each other."

"What kind of signal do you want?" Fender asked. "Smoke? Semaphore? How about a baseball catcher kind of thing?"

Rodney stared at him. "What are you talking about?"

"How about this?" Fender thought out loud. "Kaa! Kaa! Kaa!" he squawked.

A group of guests turned around to stare. "Perfect," he

muttered. "Let's get to work."

As Fender walked off to mingle with Loretta, a good-looking, slinky female bot, Rodney looked around. He didn't see Bigweld anywhere. Rodney sure hoped he would show up eventually.

Over by the buffet tables, Cappy was trapped in a conversation with Ratchet. It was almost more than she could endure.

"You know, Cappy, it's nice that you can see me away from work," he said in a flirtatious tone. "See my more casual, fun-loving side." He playfully tossed a snack in the air, caught it triumphantly in his mouth, and promptly began to choke.

Cappy took that opportunity to slip away. She glanced over her shoulder to make sure Ratchet didn't notice where she was going and ended up bumping into Rodney.

"Hey, I know you!" she said when she recognized him. "You're the flying kid."

"I am?" Rodney replied. "I mean—"

"You know, I've been thinking about you. You and your little whatchamacallit."

"The Wonderbot," Rodney told her.

Cappy nodded. "Pretty old-school, but clever."

"Yeah, well, if you guys get your way, I won't even be able to get parts for him," Rodney spat out. He turned and began to walk off.

"No, wait," Cappy urged. "Don't go. I think you're a talented kid. You know, if it were up to me . . ."

Before she could utter another syllable, she heard Ratchet calling out across the dance floor. "Cappy, yoo-hoo! Cappy?"

"Dance with me!" Cappy commanded.

"Huh?" Rodney asked, surprised. But he did as he was told, taking Cappy in his arms and sweeping her across the dance floor.

"I'll give you one thing, kid," Cappy whispered to him, as they moved across the room. "You've got some big bolts. You crashed this party, didn't you?"

"Yeah. Actually, I did," Rodney admitted.

Quickly, Cappy reached out her arm, signaling someone. "Over here, please," she called.

Rodney gasped. She'd tricked him! He thought she'd liked him, but she was simply getting rid of him. "You're throwing me out?" he exclaimed.

Cappy shook her head and smiled as a waiter bot came over with a tray of drinks. She reached out and grabbed two glasses. "Relax," she said with a smile. "Here."

"Oh, thanks," Rodney said. He was about to take a sip when searching spotlights shot across the crowd. An announcer stepped onto a big stage at the front of the room. "Ladies and gentlebots, please direct your attention to the stage," he called out.

Rodney turned along with everyone else. He knew what this meant. Bigweld would soon be addressing the crowd. This was his chance to finally meet Bigweld.

"Oh, excuse me. Sorry. I'll be right back," Rodney apologized to Cappy. He left her on the dance floor and began pushing his way through the crowd of bots.

But it wasn't Bigweld who took the stage—it was Phineas T. Ratchet! "Thank you," Ratchet said to the crowd, as they obediently applauded. "We now come to the point in the evening where I have the honor of introducing our beloved founder, Mr. Bigweld."

"Hurrah!" the crowd cheered and applauded wildly. And this time, they meant it.

"Who is," Ratchet continued, "unfortunately, unable to attend."

Rodney stopped dead in his tracks. "What?"

"He sends his apologies," Ratchet assured everyone, "his love, and a small box of assorted cookies."

"Not coming?" Rodney shouted. "He has to come." In his state of disbelief, Rodney had forgotten that he was trying to blend in with the crowd.

Ratchet's eyes were drawn right to him. "You!" he barked. "What are you doing here?"

Rodney was in trouble now. But somehow he gathered the courage to answer right back. "I came to see Bigweld," he declared.

"You want your money back?" Ratchet sneered.

Rodney refused to be intimidated. This was too important. "How come we never see him anymore?" he demanded.

A murmur went through the crowd. They'd been wondering the same thing.

Ratchet wasn't about to answer questions from someone like Rodney. He snapped his fingers to summon security. "We have a party crasher," he told them.

"That's right," Rodney told the crowd, as he pulled off the tin cans he'd used to cover his body. "I had to put on all this junk to get in here, so I could tell Bigweld that you are outmoding millions of bots. And I know because I spend all day fixing them."

"You!"

Ratchet's eyes closed into tiny, furious slits. So this was the bot who was ruining his plan—and making his mother mad.

As Ratchet's guards grabbed for Rodney, the frightened bot let out a call for help. "Kaa! Kaa!" he cried out. "Kaa! Kaa!"

Fender heard his call. He turned to Loretta, the beautiful bot he'd been dancing with all night.

"Oh, my darling," he murmured in her ear. "That is the cry of the deep doo-doo bird. I must fly!" With that, he turned and headed for Rodney.

As the security guards led Rodney from the room, Ratchet whispered an ominous demand. "Take him for a drive. Bring me back his exact weight in paper clips!"

Fortunately for Rodney, Ratchet hadn't whispered

quietly enough. Cappy had heard every word. "No!" she protested.

At that moment, everything stopped. No one at Bigweld Industries had ever said no to Ratchet before. Even he couldn't believe his ears.

"No?" he demanded threateningly.

"I mean . . ." Cappy continued, moving closer to him and speaking in a low voice few could hear, "I'll escort him out. You don't want to look bad in front of your people, do you?"

Ratchet wasn't quite sure what to think, until Cappy moved closer to him and smiled flirtatiously. "When I get back, I can show you my casual fun-loving side."

Now Ratchet was completely flustered. "Well, I . . ." he began, blushing madly.

Cappy didn't wait for a response. She pushed Rodney hard in the back. "Get moving!"

Rodney was shocked. Cappy had seemed so wonderful on the dance floor. "What are you doing?" he demanded.

"Saving your life," Cappy assured him. She tried to hurry him out the doors.

But Fender got in the way. He leaped in front of them,

blocking their path to the door. "Unhand him," he demanded of Cappy.

"Get out of here, you idiot," Cappy insisted. With a single sweep of her arm, she knocked the skinny bot to the ground and hopped over him.

Just then, Ratchet came to his senses. "She's with him!" he shouted to the guards. "Seize them."

The guards bounced to attention. They ran toward Cappy and Rodney. Ratchet followed closely behind. But they were suddenly blocked by a line of conga dancers who were parading around the floor, led by the Wonderbot. Ratchet was forced to join the dancers, and they wouldn't let him go.

Rodney grabbed Cappy and Fender by the wrists and pulled them toward the exit. The Wonderbot left the conga line and flew into Rodney's arms.

"Wait, you know him?" Cappy asked, nodding at Fender as they ran.

This was no time for formal introductions, but Rodney did his best. "Cappy, Fender. Fender, Cappy."

Ratchet wasn't the only one who wanted to stop the trio. Loretta wasn't going to let the bot of her dreams disappear so easily either. "Fenderbilt!" she cried out. "Wait for me!"

Fender decided to return to the ball with Loretta. Meanwhile, Rodney and Cappy managed to make a smooth getaway and were now driving along in Cappy's car. As the car flew over the brightly lit buildings of Robot City, Rodney looked out the window, absorbing the view. "That was amazing!" he said to Cappy. "The way you just thought of that . . ."

"You know, that was the most fun I've ever had at one of those parties," Cappy said, as she gleefully gasped for breath. "In fact, the only fun."

"Burp." The Wonderbot, who had obviously had a bit too much to drink at the party, belched from the backseat of the car.

"So, where are we going?"

"Home."

"What?" Rodney exclaimed. "No way!"

Cappy turned to look at him. "This is for your own good. You don't know what you're dealing with here. Ratchet wants to use your head as a hood ornament."

"I'm not going back," Rodney declared. "I can't give up. I made a deal with my father and—"

"Wow," Cappy interrupted him. "Is he an inventor, too?"

"He's a dishwasher," Rodney told her.

"A dish—"

"That's right!" Rodney told her defensively. "He washes dishes in a restaurant."

"Hey, take it easy," Cappy replied. "My dad's a vacuum cleaner. And my mom's the attachment set. That's how they met."

Rodney found that hard to believe. Cappy was so sophisticated. "But you, well, you don't seem like . . ."

"You didn't know me in high school," Cappy assured him. "Braces, glasses . . . I was little Cappy Ann Cappadorkus. I even had a Bigweld thinking cap."

"Hey, I still have mine!"

Cappy looked over at him and chuckled. "Well, now that's just sad."

Rodney laughed despite himself. He looked appreciatively at Cappy. She really was beautiful. Not a dork anymore. Which made him wonder . . .

"What?" she asked, after he'd been staring at her for what seemed quite a long time.

"How did you become so . . . ?"

"Upgrades," she said with a simple shrug. "Makes it easier to fit in."

Easier to fit in. "Maybe I should get some," he said.

Cappy stared at him. "You're fine," she assured him sincerely.

Rodney looked away. He was flattered and a bit flustered. He didn't know what to say.

Cappy stopped the car suddenly. "We're here," she told him, almost sadly.

But Rodney refused to get out of the car. He hadn't gotten what he'd come for. Not by a long shot. And he wasn't getting on any train until he did. "Look, I'm not leaving until I meet Bigweld," he insisted.

Cappy was shocked. "That's not—" she began.

But Rodney refused to take no for an answer. "Well, why not? You're a big shot, aren't you? You could take me . . ."

Cappy shook her head vehemently. "Nobody at the company sees Bigweld except Mr. Ratchet," she explained. "You don't think I want to see Bigweld? He's my hero, too, you know. You think I don't hate what's happening?"

"Do you?" Rodney asked her accusingly.

"Yes," Cappy assured him. "But if I got caught trying to see Bigweld—and bringing you along—I'd lose everything. My job, my future. I'd be nothing again, like . . ."

Rodney nodded. He understood now. He knew what she meant. "Like me," he said quietly.

Cappy looked away and didn't answer. Rodney understood. He opened the car door and stepped out into the night. But he couldn't leave without letting her know exactly how he felt. "Next time you upgrade yourself, check out the catalog and see if it sells a conscience." He closed the car door and walked off.

After a moment, Cappy pulled the car up beside him and lowered the window. "Get in."

CHAPTER TEN

Fender had no idea that Rodney was off on an adventure with Cappy. He had been spending a lovely evening with Loretta at the ball. Now it was time to say good night.

"Oh, my darling," he said as he kissed Loretta's hand. Loretta giggled like a schoolgirl.

"Thanks for walking me home," she said.

"Thanks for carrying me up that hill," Fender replied.

"Until tomorrow?"

Fender sighed. "I shall count the seconds." He paused for a moment. "So far, I'm up to four."

"You crazy nut." Loretta laughed.

"Crazy about you," Fender assured her.

Loretta squealed with delight and then raced into her house.

"Ooooh." Fender sighed happily as he kicked up his heels and began to dance his way home. His metal feet clunked against the sidewalk, giving him the perfect beat to sing to.

"I'm singin' in the oil. Just singin' in the oil!" He grabbed a lamppost and swung around, clicking his heels with pure delight.

The lamppost was not amused. "Get your hands off me," she demanded.

The mailbox on the corner didn't appreciate Fender's hands-on behavior either. "That's my wife, buddy," he warned angrily.

Fender looked at the tall, slender lamppost, and the short, squat mailbox. "Woopsie daisy," Fender said. "Sorry. But just like you two crazy kids, I'm in love. From now on, I'm a winner."

Or maybe not.

Whoosh! Suddenly a sweeper swept by, its jaws open. In a split second, it completely consumed the Rusty.

"Wait! This is a big mistake!" Fender cried from inside the sweeper. "Let me out! Do I look like an outmode to you?"

It was dark and cramped inside the sweeper. Fender could hear strange noises coming from outside. "Open the doors!" He

Rodney Copperbottom wants to be a great inventor like his hero, Bigweld.

Just like Bigweld says, "See a need, fill a need."

Rodney arrives at the gate of Bigweld Industries to meet Bigweld.

Instead, he finds Phineas T. Ratchet in charge.

Rodney wrestles with Fender to get his foot back.

At Aunt Fan's, all bots are welcome!

Madame Gasket plots with Ratchet to turn old bots into scrap metal.

Rodney and the Rusties wonder: Can they afford upgrades?

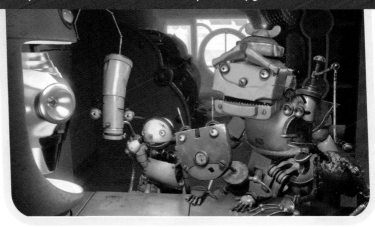

Bots everywhere are falling apart!

Rodney gets some advice from Bigweld.

Oh, no! Fender is sweeper bait!

Will Fender escape from the Chop Shop?

Bigweld is back . . .

. . . and Ratchet is in trouble!

The Super Rusties are ready to take back Robot City.

Bigweld was right: "You can shine no matter what you're made of."

banged angrily on the jaws of the sweeper. "Open the doors!"

As if on command, the sweeper's jaws opened, revealing the dark dungeon that was the Chop Shop. It was truly an awful sight to behold.

"Close the doors!" Fender shouted. "Close the doors!"

The sweeper tilted upward and spilled its entire contents, including Fender, onto the floor.

"Aaaaaaaaahhhhhh!" Fender shouted, as he tumbled onto a long conveyor belt that moved through the factory.

Fender's fear soon turned to glee, as he rolled along past piles and piles of spare parts. He reached out excitedly and grabbed all the hands, feet, noses, and eyes from the spare part smorgasbord that he could hold. "Wow!" he exclaimed. "Look at all these parts. So many things I've wanted all my life." He spotted a particularly attractive body part in the piles. "Oh, that's pretty!" he cried, as he reached out his hand.

Snap! A saw blade came down right in front of him. Fender screamed and snatched his hand back just in time. Suddenly, he remembered the danger he was in. He looked around and spotted a group of Madame Gasket's minions standing around a grinder.

Yikes! He had to get out of there!

The petrified Rusty jumped up and tried to run in the opposite direction. Like a kid going the wrong way on an escalator, Fender was fighting a losing battle. But he was determined to get away. He kept running, hoping against hope that his rickety body could outrace the conveyor belt. Unfortunately, as he tried to run, his foot got caught in a spring on the mechanism. He struggled to pull himself free, but it was no use.

Suddenly, a fresh load of street-swept spare parts fell from the ceiling and began heading straight for Fender. He was certain to be buried alive.

Bam! A huge piece of metal slammed against Fender, knocking him off the conveyor belt. "Yaaaaahhhhh!" he screamed, as he bungeed off the belt and swung toward the ground, his foot still stuck in that darn spring. Fender hovered upside down over the lower level of the Chop Shop. He moved along slowly with the conveyor belt, unable to wrest himself from the spring.

Just then, Fender heard Ratchet's voice coming from below him. He looked over, and got a clear—if upside down—view of Ratchet speaking to a horrifying looking woman.

"Okay, Mother. This way," Ratchet was saying.

Fender gasped.

"Oh, I can't bear it," Madame Gasket replied. "Let me look, let me look. Oh please. . . ." Her hands were over her eyes, and her hideous body was practically quivering with anticipation as her son turned her around.

"No peeking now," Ratchet teased playfully. "It's a surprise."

"Oh, you are a wicked boy."

By now, even Fender was dying to see what the big surprise was. He didn't have to wait long.

"And look!" Ratchet told his mother.

The old bot lowered her hands and gasped. Her eyes filled with drops of oil. But they were tears of joy. Her son had given her a wonderful gift—a new model sweeper, bigger and shinier and more vicious than the older ones. Best of all, it had a custom license plate that read PSYKO MAMA.

"For me," Madame Gasket murmured gratefully.

Ratchet held up the keys. "It's got a full tank of gas! If you're ready to mow, she's ready to go. I figure if we're gonna do it, let's do it right."

Madame Gasket looked proudly at her son. "Has any mother ever had a better son?" she asked.

"Ah, thanks Mom." Ratchet said, trying not to sound too pleased. "Oh, by the way, I found out who's been fixing those outmodes." He used a fancy remote control to open the sweeper's jaws. "So starting tomorrow, these babies will be rounding up him and anyone else in a five-mile radius."

Hanging upside down while caught in a spring is not the best way to hear your friend is about to be eliminated by a horde of evil machines. Fender stifled a cry as he clawed at his spring, trying to get further away from the evil duo.

His nightmare was about to get worse. At that very moment, Ratchet and his mother looked upward and spotted Fender hanging overhead. And they were not pleased to find an outmode hanging around.

"What the . . . !" Madame Gasket shouted out. She leaped toward Fender, grabbing in his direction. The conveyor belt continued moving, and he was yanked out of her reach in the nick of time.

"Aaaaah!" Fender cried out, as he was carried away.

Madame Gasket let out a particularly sinister laugh. It always made her happy when another rusty, outmoded bot made its way into the grinder.

The spring holding Fender's foot jerked up so suddenly that it ripped the bottom half of his body right off, and Fender fell back onto the conveyor belt. The shock was overwhelming. But Fender couldn't cry over his spilled legs right now. The conveyor belt was moving closer and closer to the grinder. Fender grabbed the nearest set of legs and attached them to his torso. When he looked down, he realized he'd given himself a pair of woman's legs, complete with a skirt and high heels.

"This is so wrong! This is so wrong!" Fender complained, as he studied his new lower half. Fender hobbled on his stiletto heels until he reached the end of the conveyor belt, and then jumped to safety. He landed in a Dumpster. As he popped his head up from the collected junk, he noticed that a few springs and coils had attached themselves to his head. "Help!" he shouted, as he darted out of the Chop Shop as quickly as his new high heels could carry him.

CHAPTER ELEVEN

Cappy quietly parked her car on a platform outside Bigweld's massive mansion. She was careful not to make a sound as she stepped out of the car and closed the door. Rodney and the Wonderbot followed her, moving silently across the lawn and up to the huge front door.

Cappy looked around. There was a pile of old newspapers and uncollected mail on the front stoop. "Okay, we tried," Cappy said. "Let's get outta here."

But Rodney wasn't willing to give up so easily. "No, something's up. Look at all these newspapers and this mail."

"Oh, come on," Cappy argued. "They probably stopped delivering these years ago."

Just then a paperboy bot threw a rolled up newspaper at the

stoop. It slammed right into Cappy's face.

Rodney laughed. He liked being proven right.

But Cappy had a little surprise for Rodney, too. She showed him the front page of the paper. There was Rodney's picture, right in the center. The headline read BAD BOT BUSTS BALL.

"A nice photograph of you," Cappy mused, studying the picture. She looked him straight in the eye. "Come on. We gotta get you out of here."

But Rodney wasn't going anywhere. Bravely, he pushed the door open. It creaked loudly. The Wonderbot shivered and closed up like a clam.

Cappy shuddered. "Big creaky door." She moaned. "Perfect."

Bigweld's house was anything but warm and inviting, as Rodney had imagined it would be. Instead, it was huge and foreboding. There was no sign that brilliant inventions had ever been created here. The place was completely lifeless.

The blackness of the entry hall enveloped Rodney and Cappy. Their eyes glowed in the dark like four flashlights, illuminating the rooms as they wandered through. Suddenly, Rodney's eyes focused on the very place he'd dreamed about since he was a tiny bot. Rodney couldn't control his excitement.

"Oh, wow!" he exclaimed. "Look at this! This is Bigweld's actual workshop! I recognize it from his old TV show."

"Could you keep it down?" Cappy shushed him. "We're not supposed to be here."

But Rodney's enthusiasm would not be curbed. He flopped down onto a huge desk chair and wheeled himself over to the far wall, where a series of blackboards revealed some of Bigweld's work.

"Do you know what these are?" he asked with a boyish glee that Cappy couldn't help but smile at. "These are Bigweld's original designs. That's his own writing!"

Cappy pulled a book from the shelf and started turning the pages. She became confused as she paged further into the volume. "This is strange," she mused out loud. "How come the writing just stops in the middle? And there's oil all over this page." She turned a few pages. "And the rest are all blank."

But Rodney wasn't listening. He'd discovered something else in the room that caught his fancy. A huge row of dominoes sat on a nearby table. "Remember? He used to have these on his shows."

Cappy looked over at him sadly. Something was very wrong. The dripped oil was not a good sign. "Uh, Rodney," she began, "I don't know how to tell you this . . ."

"Why are they so dusty?" Rodney thought aloud, as he studied the dominoes. He leaned over to blow some of the dust from the small tiles.

"Wait!" Cappy cried out. "Don't!"

"Oops," Rodney muttered sheepishly.

"Quick, stop those!" Cappy warned as the first domino tipped over. "Someone will know we're here."

But it was too late. Once the first domino fell, the others followed. The row of dominoes led out the door and around the corner. Rodney and Cappy followed the falling tiles, frantically trying to stop the cascade.

The trail led them into an immense room filled with nothing but dominoes. Rodney's mouth dropped open in surprise. There was a massive domino structure in the middle of the floor—at least a million tiny tiles had been placed in varying rows and tiers. It was an unbelievably complex design, mechanically and technically brilliant. There was only one bot clever enough to have created it—Bigweld. Rodney and Cappy stared at the dominoes.

"Whoa! This is much more elaborate than the ones on his show," Rodney exclaimed.

"Oh, no!" Cappy cried out, as lines of dominoes toppled around them. The tiles were getting bigger and bigger!

"Ohhh!"

"Oh, no!"

Cappy and Rodney both cried out in fear as they darted out of the way of a monster-sized domino that was about to crush them. At the last moment, Rodney went back and pulled the Wonderbot out of the way of an oncoming domino tsunami.

"Aah!" Rodney shouted out.

"Ugh!" Cappy added.

"Whoa!" they screamed together.

"Help!" Cappy shouted, desperate to be heard over the powerful volume of the domino avalanche.

"There's no use screaming," Rodney told her, raising the volume of his voice as well. "We're the only ones here."

Before Cappy could respond, the doors to the workshop burst open. The two frightened bots gasped. They couldn't believe their eyes. There he was—Bigweld! Cappy and Rodney watched in amazement as he burst into the room and surfed over the sea of dominoes on a bizarre domino surfboard, catching the waves and riding them with ease—until one wave got too strong for the large-sized inventor. Wipe out!

Rodney and Cappy made their way over to the big guy, who was lying motionless on the ground.

"Is it really him?" Rodney asked.

"It looks like him," Cappy said. "Is he dead?"

Cautiously, Rodney reached down and poked at his large belly. Instantly, Bigweld sat up, fully alert. He shook his head for a moment, as if to get some water out of his ears.

"Watch out for the undertow!" Bigweld told them, looking at the huge collection of fallen dominoes surrounding him. "Whoo!"

"Are you all right?" Cappy asked him nervously.

"Considering I'm an old fat guy who crashed onto the floor, I'm fantastic!" Bigweld assured her as he jumped up onto his feet. "Come on! Let's set 'em up again. Only bigger!"

Rodney looked triumphantly at Cappy. "He doesn't look dead," he said.

"You two start on that end!" Bigweld shouted excitedly. "I'll check back with you in a year!"

Rodney nervously cleared his throat. This was his chance to talk to Bigweld about all the terrible things he'd seen since he'd arrived in Robot City. "Mr. Bigweld," he began.

"Talking isn't building," the big man interrupted him.

"Is this what you've been working on?" Rodney asked him incredulously. "This is why no one sees you?"

Bigweld, looked up, annoyed at the interruption. "Young man, nobody likes a chatterbox," he scolded Rodney. He went back to work on his new domino creation.

"But there's a terrible crisis, Mr. Bigweld," Rodney told him.

Bigweld stood up and looked understandingly into Rodney's eyes. "I know," he told him sincerely.

Rodney breathed a sigh of relief.

"We're working without music," Bigweld observed.

Rodney frowned as Bigweld pushed a button on a CD player. The sound of piano music rushed forth. "That's me on the piano," Bigweld boasted. He sat back down and set up a fresh row of dominoes.

"We need to talk!" Rodney shouted at him, desperate to be heard over the music.

As Bigweld looked up at the anxious bot, his big arm knocked over the new row of tiles. He shook his head. "Son, I've got to tell you, you're making a lousy first impression."

Cappy hurried to intervene. "Please, sir," she pleaded. "He's your biggest fan. In fact, he's an inventor like you."

"Well," Rodney began sheepishly.

But Cappy wouldn't allow him to be modest. "Show him that thing you made," she insisted.

That caught Bigweld's attention. "A device?" he asked excitedly. "A doohickey? A thingamajig?"

"Yes." Rodney nodded.

"Not interested," Bigweld said. He turned back to his dominoes.

"But—" Rodney protested.

"All right." Bigweld sighed. "I see we're not going to accomplish anything until we get this over with." He shot Rodney a bored glance and flopped down onto one of his oversized seats. "Okay, thrill me."

Nervously, Rodney held up the Wonderbot. "Now, don't be scared," he told his invention in a calm, soothing voice. "Show Mr. Bigweld what you can do."

Rodney flipped on the Wonderbot. They all stared at the small creature. But it did nothing. And then, suddenly . . . boom!

It exploded.

"Is that what it's supposed to do?" Bigweld asked.

"It gets nervous under pressure," Rodney explained.

Bigweld stood and placed one of his gigantic arms around Rodney's small shoulders. "Son, let me give you a good piece of advice . . ."

"Yes?" Rodney perked up, anxious to hear any helpful hints his idol might bestow upon him.

"Give up."

"What?!" he demanded. "You're telling me to quit?"

Bigweld shook his head. "I said, 'give up,'" he corrected Rodney. "But 'quit' works just as well."

Rodney was stunned. "Is that what you did? Is that why you're sitting here letting Ratchet turn robots into outmodes?"

Bigweld shrugged. "Kid, sometimes you've just got to know when you're licked, when the problem's too big and you're not bot enough to fix it."

"But you're Bigweld," Rodney reminded him. "You can fix anything."

"I used to think so." Bigweld sighed. "But times change. The world got shinier and faster. I became old-fashioned. An out-mode. Ratchet's the future, I'm the past. At least that's what every-body out there thinks. Except this pathetic little dreamer here." He looked pointedly at Rodney. "Go home, kid. If it beat me, it's gonna beat you."

"But—" Rodney interrupted.

Bigweld shook his head. "The world you're looking for no longer exists. You missed it. Find some other foolish dream." The big bot picked up a few of his fallen dominoes. "Now if you'll excuse me, I'm very, uh, busy."

Rodney looked stricken. The sympathy he had begun to feel for Bigweld disappeared. He was left with a mix of emptiness and resentment. "Yeah, I can see that," he murmured. Then he turned to Cappy. "You were right. You can take me to the train station now. Bigweld is dead."

Bigweld didn't even bother to look up as his front door slammed shut.

CHAPTER TWELVE

Cappy walked up to the ticket window at the Robot City para-train station. "Rivet Town, please," she said to the ticket bot. "One way."

The ticket bot spit a single ticket from his mouth. Cappy snatched it from his jaws and walked over to a nearby phone booth. Rodney was inside, calling home.

"Hi, Mom. It's me, Rodney," he said into the receiver. His mother asked how he was doing, and Rodney couldn't help but lie. "I'm doing fine. How are you and Dad?"

"He's right here," Mrs. Copperbottom said. "I'll put him on." She handed the phone to her husband.

"Hey, buddy, how's it going?" the old dishwasher asked his son excitedly.

Rodney hated lying to his father. So he avoided the question completely by quickly changing the topic to his father's health.

"I'm fine, fine," Mr. Copperbottom assured his son. But his deep, throaty cough was proof enough that Rodney wasn't the only one lying. "I've just been a little under the weather. We're having some trouble finding your old man a replacement part, that's all. He stopped for a moment, not wanting to burden Rodney with his troubles. "Hey, let's talk about you. What kind of work are you doing? What's Bigweld like? Did you meet him?"

"Yeah, Dad, I . . . I met him. But . . ."

"What's wrong, son?" Mr. Copperbottom asked gently.

Rodney paused for a moment, collecting his thoughts. "It's . . . not how we thought it was, Dad," he said, struggling to put his feelings into words. "I'm not . . . I haven't . . . I can't . . ."

Mr. Copperbottom understood. He and Rodney didn't need many words to communicate their thoughts. "I see," the dishwasher said slowly.

"I'm really sorry, Dad," Rodney apologized. "I'm sorry I let you down."

"No, no, no, you could never let me down," Mr.

Copperbottom hurried to assure his only child. "I just wanted, so much, for things to be different for you from the way they were for . . ." He stopped himself. This was no time for self-pity. "Listen, I know it isn't easy Rodney, but a dream you don't fight for can haunt you for the rest of your life."

"Yeah, Dad," Rodney said slowly. He wished he could believe his father, but right now, it all seemed so hopeless.

"I love you, boy," Herb Copperbottom said, as he ended the conversation.

As he hung up the phone, Rodney felt completely drained.

"Your father loves you very much," the phone booth said to him.

"I know," Rodney agreed wearily.

"With our Friends and Family Plan you could talk to him five hundred minutes a month, free on nights and weekends," the phone booth suggested.

Rodney wanted no part of that. He hurried out of the booth.

"Yoo-hoo! Rodney, wait! Don't go yet!"

Rodney turned and saw Aunt Fan waddling down the train platform with his suitcase in hand. She gasped for air as she finally reached him and placed the small bag on the ground. "Your suitcase."

"Thanks, Aunt Fan," he replied. "But . . ."

Aunt Fan gasped for air. "I'm going to miss you, dear boy," she panted, trying to catch her breath. "You know the others wanted to see you off, too."

"Why didn't they?"

"Hmm? Oh, they did," she replied.

Rodney looked around, confused. There didn't seem to be anyone else on the platform. Then, Aunt Fan pressed a button on her large torso. Her giant rear end opened up, and Lug, Diesel, Piper, and Crank all fell out.

"Next time, let's split a cab." Crank moaned as he struggled to straighten up.

Cappy stood beside Rodney and looked at the Rusties. The Rusties looked back at Cappy.

"Who the heck is she?" Piper asked enviously.

"You know, I used to have a figure like that," Aunt Fan informed the Rusties. The Rusties looked at her large rear end dubiously, but didn't say anything.

Just then, a new passenger arrived at the ticket counter. It was Fender. And he was far more anxious than Rodney to get out of town.

"Hurry," Fender told the ticket bot. "One ticket to anywhere."

Fender's friends barely recognized him. They'd never seen him in a skirt and heels before. But no matter what his lower torso looked like, Fender was still Fender. And in a moment, he was surrounded by his best buddies.

"Guess what? Crank was right," he informed them. "It's the sweepers. They're rounding up outmodes and taking them—I mean us!—to Madame Gasket's Chop Shop. And guess who's really behind it all."

"Who?" Rodney asked excitedly.

Fender's face fell. "You really don't want to guess?" he asked disappointedly. "Come on. I came all this way in cha-cha heels."

Rodney thought for a moment. "Ratchet," he guessed.

"It's Ratchet," Fender revealed, completely ignoring Rodney's guess.

"He's Madame Gasket's son! And he's built a fleet of sweepers. And they're coming after us!" Now Fender was shouting. "Listen to me! Listen to me! We won't last a week!"

The Rusties all began talking at once.

"Settle down," Crank ordered. "I've got a plan. Let's all get on that train!"

The Rusties hurried toward the ticket booth.

"Hey, wait a minute! You're all giving up?" Rodney asked them.

"You started it," Crank told him.

"Well, I'm ending it!" Rodney told him defiantly. "If I don't do something about Ratchet, no one will. We've got to figure out a way to take this city back. With or without Bigweld!"

"Fighting never solved anything," Aunt Fan reminded him.

"Quitting isn't so productive either, I gotta tell you."

Everyone turned to focus on the source of the deep, booming voice that had just emerged from behind Rodney.

"It's the big boy!" Crank gasped.

Aunt Fan looked as though she were going to faint. "Oh, be still my pump." She sighed.

Bigweld smiled at Rodney. "Kid, if you're gonna fight, I'm

going in with you." He held out his hands. The Wonderbot flew out, completely revitalized.

Rodney was amazed. Bigweld had fixed his invention.

Rodney reached out his hand. "Then let's do it!" he exclaimed, as he shook the big bot's hand.

"Come on, gang," Bigweld said. "Let's give that Ratchet an old-school fixin'. What do you say?"

The Rusties responded with an overwhelming cheer.

"Oh, what a man," Aunt Fan swooned. Then, passion overcame the big bot, and she fainted, landing squarely on Diesel.

"Someone get a crane!" Crank called out, trying to save his friend.

CHAPTER THIRTEEN

Ratchet had no idea what was in store for him as he sat in his office the following morning. But as he sipped his cool drink, and recorded yet another restrictive corporate memo, Bigweld, Rodney, Cappy, and the Rusties were on their way over to the corporate headquarters, ready to do battle.

As his gigantic limo pulled up in front of Bigweld Industries, Bigweld barked out his orders like any strong general. "Okay! Boardroom, ten minutes! I want you both there, Rodney and Cappy."

"Mr. Bigweld, should we come, too?" Lug asked excitedly.

"Uhh . . ." Bigweld looked over the rest of his troops. "No, no. You stay here and watch Daddy's limo. Right now I'm going inside to kick some corporate booty," he announced. Then he turned to Cappy. "You know, your boyfriend here's a genius."

"What?" Rodney asked, confused.

"Oh, he's not my . . ." Cappy began. Then she stopped herself. She wasn't exactly sure what her relationship with Rodney was. "Is he?"

"I am?" Rodney seconded.

Bigweld nodded. He put a strong hand on Rodney's hand-me-down shoulder. "Thanks for still believing in me," he said sincerely. Bigweld looked up at the corporate skyscraper before him and smiled for the first time in a very long while. "Ahhh, it's good to be home," he said as he strode into the building.

A few minutes later, Bigweld charged into his corporate headquarters with all the power of a steel elephant.

"It's Mr. Bigweld!" the execs gasped. Clank! A tall executive bot's jaw dropped and smashed right onto the top of the head of a smaller executive standing beneath him. Another corporate bot was so excited, he dropped his pants. "Bigweld," he murmured, as he pulled his trousers back around his waist.

The executives parted like the waves of the Red Sea and left a clear pathway for their boss. Bigweld strode with determination down the hall, stopping at the reception desk. "Tell Mr. Ratchet his ten o'clock is here," he bellowed.

"Yes, sir," the flabbergasted receptionist replied. She pushed a button on her phone and announced the big boss's arrival.

This was one call Ratchet was not happy to receive. "No . . . no . . . tell him I'm not here," Ratchet begged his receptionist frantically. "Tell him anything. I don't care. Just . . . just don't let him in."

Too late. The doors to Ratchet's office slammed open and a furious Bigweld burst in. "Ratchet!" he bellowed at an ear-shattering volume.

Ratchet let out a high-pitched scream and leaped onto a chair in fear. But Bigweld showed no mercy.

"I'll get right to the point," he declared.

"What happened?" Ratchet asked in a fast, frantic voice. "Run out of dominoes? Party ice? I'll send you some more."

But that wasn't going to do it. Not anymore. "You're fired!" Bigweld announced.

Ratchet gasped. "Fired? On what grounds? This company has never been more profitable."

Bigweld dismissed that claim with a wave of his considerably sized hand and then dumped Ratchet right out of his chair. "Profits, shmofits. Now get out!"

Ratchet fell to his knees and began to plead. "No, wait, please listen to me. You can't do this to me. This job is my life," he begged pathetically. "You don't know what I've done here. The lies I've told, the lives I've ruined." He stopped for a moment, realizing what had just come out of his mouth. "Wait, this isn't helping me."

It certainly wasn't. Bigweld had already taken back his chair, his desk, his phone, and his control of the company. "Get me security," he demanded, as he called the reception desk.

Ratchet grabbed the phone receiver from Bigweld's hand. "Wait, please!" he begged. "Can't I just make one more heartfelt plea?"

Bigweld sighed. "Okay. What do you want to say?"

Ratchet raised the receiver high and banged it down with full force onto Bigweld's head. "That!" he shouted with insane glee.

Bigweld collapsed to the floor unconscious. Ratchet stood there for a moment, looking down at him. Even he was surprised by the violence he was capable of. "Oh, my God," he murmured. "I'm as crazy as my mother."

"Awwww . . ." Bigweld moaned in pain.

Instinctively, Ratchet bashed him in the head again. Madame Gasket would have been proud.

A few minutes later, four burly guards were slowly walking a very woozy Bigweld toward the elevator. "Take fatface to the Chop Shop," Ratchet ordered. "We don't need him anymore."

But it wasn't going to be that easy. Not if Rodney, Cappy, and the Wonderbot had anything to do with it. They arrived at the boardroom just in time to see Bigweld being taken away. The Wonderbot moved in quickly, tripping two of the guards and knocking the other two guards' heads together.

Without the guards to hold him up, Bigweld crashed to the floor with a thud. Instantly, Rodney jumped onto his back. The Wonderbot flew behind them and gave Bigweld a giant push. They started rolling down the hallway toward the elevator door.

But they soon realized that a crowd of executives had gathered there, and Rodney and Bigweld would not be able to get through quickly enough. There was only one thing to do.

Crash! Rodney, Bigweld, and the Wonderbot smashed through the top-floor window. The Wonderbot grabbed onto

Rodney and struggled to fly both him and Bigweld to safety. But the weight of the big guy was too much for the little Wonderbot to handle and he dropped them. They plummeted to the ground.

Worse yet, Ratchet was hot on their trail. "Get him!" he ordered his security guards. "Kill him! Crush him!"

Ratchet was so determined to make sure Rodney didn't escape again that he himself started running after him. But he didn't get very far before he tripped over a dainty little outstretched foot. "Oof." He groaned as he fell to the floor with a thud. He looked up and eyed the culprit. "Cappy! Did you do that to me?!"

"Oops, that was an accident," Cappy said in a small, frightened voice.

Ratchet smiled triumphantly. But his joy was short-lived.

"I meant to do this," Cappy continued, kicking him hard in the butt.

"Awwggh!" Ratchet moaned.

Cappy didn't wait around to gloat. Rodney needed her. She clicked her heels twice, and small wheels popped out from the soles of her shoes. She took off after Rodney and Bigweld.

Ratchet wasn't the only bot in pain. Rodney and Bigweld

weren't doing much better after their big drop from the top of the building.

"Mr. Bigweld," Rodney asked his idol. "Are you okay?"

Bigweld looked at him through glazed, unfocused eyes. "Fatface to the Chop Shop," he sang. "Fatface to the Chop Shop."

"I'll take that as a no." Rodney sighed.

The Rusties were waiting to find out what would happen next. Of course, they had no idea what had just occurred in the boardroom, because they were busy keeping themselves from getting bored. They'd turned on the limo's TVs and were bouncing up and down on the seats, all to the musical accompaniment of Diesel, who was playing a tune on the car horn. They'd turned the limo into a party on wheels.

"Road trip, road trip, road trip!" Crank, Lug, and Fender chanted, as they stood up and poked their heads out through the sunroof.

Piper seemed to be the only one keeping her mind on the task at hand. She poked her head out of the window, just to yell at her brother and his friends. "You guys are so embarrassing," she began. But she stopped just in time to see Rodney go rolling by on top of Bigweld. Ratchet's men were in hot pursuit. "That was Rodney!" she called to the others. "He's in some kind of trouble."

Piper wasn't kidding. At that very moment, a security bot was about to grab Rodney. Luckily, Cappy was ready for him. With one well-aimed punch, she knocked the guard into a fountain, giving Rodney and Bigweld just enough time to roll safely out the front gate. She tried to chase after Rodney, but a giant magnet truck swerved out of nowhere, almost knocking her to the ground. By the time the truck had cleared away, Rodney and Bigweld had rolled on.

It was clear they needed help, and Piper figured she was just the girl to come to their aid. "Come on!" she ordered. "We've got to help Rodney."

But her brother wasn't about to allow that. "No, Piper, you stay here," he told her.

"No way."

"Let's be honest. We're headed for a huge butt-whuppin'. Please, stay here and whatever happens—make something of yourself. You're the only thing I've got to leave behind."

There was nothing more to say. Piper got out of the car and stood beside Aunt Fan. Together, they watched as the car full of Rusties rode off into battle.

"He's right," Aunt Fan told Piper as the Rusties drove off. "They're headed for a huge butt-whuppin'."

Piper sighed. It had to be the truth. After all, who knew more about huge butts than Aunt Fan?

Rodney had no idea that the Rusties were rushing to his aid. All he knew was that Bigweld needed his help. The scientific genius's mind was complete mush. The bot who had once played beautiful classical piano music was now perfectly happy singing a childhood song over and over.

"If you're happy and you know it, clap your hands. If you're happy and you know it, clap your hands . . ." he sang out.

Rodney glanced behind him just in time to see a fleet of magnet trucks coming after them. Quickly, he steered Bigweld off the road. Together they turned onto a crosstown street. They rolled on . . . against traffic! Car pods were flying toward them, and no one seemed to want to stop for the rolling inventors. It was up to Rodney to steer Bigweld. He swerved the big guy back and forth, dodging the oncoming pods, and finally landing them on an empty piece of road. There, they were out of danger.

At least for the moment.

That was going to have to be good enough. Rodney opened Bigweld's skull and nimbly began rewiring him, hoping to correct the brain damage.

"Daisy, Daisy, give me your answer true . . . ," Bigweld sang happily, as Rodney poked and prodded in his head.

Rodney switched a few connections, straightened some wires, and then quickly closed up Bigweld's skull. "Got it," he mumbled to himself.

Bigweld's eyes focused almost immediately. He sat up and looked around. "Rodney, what's going on?" he asked. "Where are we?"

"It's okay," Rodney said with a sigh of relief. "You're all right."

Whoosh! A magnet truck swerved alongside them, and sucked Bigweld and Rodney up onto its magnet. Rodney had spoken too soon. Nothing was all right. Ratchet had captured them, Rodney was sure of it. But then he realized the driver of this truck was Cappy. She turned around and waved happily at Rodney.

Before Rodney could wave back, another magnet grabbed him and Bigweld. They were pulled toward a second truck. And that one really was being driven by Ratchet.

Still, Cappy wasn't giving up. She sped along at top speed, trying to free Rodney and Bigweld. But Ratchet kept the pace. Before long, both magnet trucks were playing a petrifying game of tug-of-war—using Rodney and Bigweld as the rope!

But help was on its way! Bigweld's limo, populated with a small troop of dedicated Rusties, was gaining on Ratchet's truck. Swiftly, they opened the sunroof. Lug lifted Diesel, Crank, and Fender through the opening.

"Rodney, grab me!" Fender called out, as he strained toward Rodney and Bigweld. But the magnetic force of Ratchet's truck got to the Rusties before Rodney could. They were yanked from the limo, and, instantly, their bodies formed a single, rusty, magnetic ball around Rodney and Bigweld.

Now Ratchet had all his enemies in one place. With a swift turn of the wheel, he bumped Cappy's truck off the road and into another lane.

But Ratchet hadn't considered the force of the magnet on Cappy's truck. Because the Rodney–Bigweld–Rusties ball was still attached to both magnets, Cappy too was dragged away. The two magnet trucks traveled side by side for a few feet, and then, suddenly, the road split in two. Cappy's truck headed down one side of the fork. Ratchet's moved along the other. Rodney, Bigweld, and the Rusties were caught in the middle!

As painful as that was, Rodney got the opportunity to get a good look at Ratchet's truck. He made a wonderful discovery— there was a plug on Ratchet's magnet! If he could just pull that plug . . .

The Rusties had spread out between the two magnet trucks, so Rodney walked gingerly across the outstretched Rusties as if they were a tightrope. He reached for the plug with his wrench. But Ratchet spotted him. There was no way he was letting his magnet go. He put the pedal to the metal and began to speed off.

But Rodney was just as quick. With one swift turn of his wrist, he released the magnet plug on Ratchet's truck. Wham! The Rusties and Bigweld slammed onto the magnet on Cappy's truck. They were safe . . .

Or were they?

The Rusties' cheers were short-lived. Cappy had been so busy moving away from Ratchet, she hadn't noticed where she was heading. The Chop Shop was right in front of them!

Cappy thought fast and turned the wheel to steer the truck away. Out of nowhere, a pair of evil sweepers appeared, surprising her. She tried to turn again, but there was nowhere to go. Smash! The magnet truck crashed into the wall of the Chop Shop.

When the smoke from the crash cleared, Rodney, Cappy, and the Rusties found themselves standing in a huge pile of junk and spare parts. Bigweld was nowhere to be seen.

"That's it. Game over" said Crank, throwing his hands up in despair.

But Rodney wasn't ready to give up. He started digging through the pile. "This is our moment to shine. This is where you show what you're really made of." He was trying to boost their spirits, but Fender, who had just fallen off the magnet truck and into the pile of junk, was not easy to convince.

"In my case, that's a rare metal called afraidium." He retorted.

But Crank was beginning to get the message. "Rodney's right! I am tired of just complaining and never doing anything. I . . . I . . . I want to try." Rodney looked up, pleased, but then Crank continued, "No, forget it, I'm sorry . . ." Rodney went back to work. "No! Yes!" Crank couldn't make up his mind.

"You're first, Crank." Rodney made the executive decision. He rolled a huge tire up to the confused bot.

"First for what?" Lug asked.

"For an upgrade!" Rodney announced, pulling out his tools.

CHAPTER FOURTEEN

As far as Madame Gasket was concerned, Bigweld would be the first to go. It took considerable effort, but she was able to stuff him into a giant cauldron attached to a high-wire on her ceiling. The cauldron moved along the wire, closer and closer to the fiery grinder that would eventually destroy the once powerful robot.

"Gasket, you are a sick, twisted, evil robot!" Bigweld shouted.

But Madame Gasket seemed to take it as a compliment. "I try," she replied modestly.

Just as Bigweld was about to be chomped by the grinder, his cauldron came to an abrupt stop. Bigweld peered over the edge and was shocked to see Rodney and the Wonderbot wedging a metal rod in the gears. They had saved him!

Behind Rodney, Bigweld thought he saw the rest of the Rusties coming into the Chop Shop, but they sure didn't look like the Rusties he was used to. Crank was souped-up like a monster truck, and the others were actually riding on top of him! As they got closer, Bigweld was more and more amazed. The Rusties had been transformed into powerful fighting machines. Fender was now a warrior, complete with an electronic cattle prod to use as a weapon. Lug was dressed in an elaborate wrestling uniform and Diesel was decked out in cowboy gear. They were Super Rusties! Fender had told Rodney to come up with a brilliant plan and he had.

But Madame Gasket had caught sight of them, too. She walked over to where they were standing near the door. "Oh, good, company," she greeted them. "Who are you losers anyway?"

"We, sir—" Fender began to introduce himself.

"I'm a woman!" Madame Gasket screamed.

Diesel's eye lens cracked at the sound.

"We've come to rescue our friends, you evil bag of bolts! And you are about to be defeated by the very outmodes you scorn and detest!"

"Yeah!" Crank added triumphantly. "Because there are seven of us and only one of you."

Crank realized he had spoken a bit too soon when a large group of bots suddenly appeared and surrounded their evil leader.

"Okay, there's seven of us and"—Fender began counting the minions—"eight . . . nine . . ."

"Did you count that one?" Crank asked, pointing to another behind Madame Gasket.

"I think so," Fender replied. But he wasn't sure. "Could you all stop moving around?" he asked them. "It's so frustrating. I know I counted one of you twice . . ."

"While you're at it, count these," Madame Gasket said, smiling.

An alarm rang out in the Chop Shop while a door opened revealing an army of new high-end sweepers. Ratchet rode in on the lead sweeper, like a general at the head of a glistening army.

Madame Gasket let out an evil laugh. "As soon as they're done with you, these sweepers will hit the streets."

"This is the last day any outmode will ever see," Ratchet added. The fleet of five sweepers moved into formation behind him. Rodney, Cappy, and the Rusties knew they were outnumbered. They shot panicked looks at each other, but no one had any ideas.

Just then, a loud sawing sound came from the wall behind the Rusties. A circle was being cut out of the wall! Clang! The circle fell to the ground. Piper stepped through the hole. "Am I too late for the butt-whuppin'?" she asked.

"Um . . . no," the Rusties assured her. "As a matter of fact, you're a little bit early," Crank said.

Then Piper stepped aside and revealed the most beautiful sight the Rusties had ever seen: All the outmodes Rodney had fixed were there to help him now. They were spinning their wrenches, ready to rid the world of Madame Gasket and her Chop Shop.

Piper smiled. "Well, let's get it started!"

The outmodes poured down the ramps of the Chop Shop. The battle was on. Aunt Fan knocked down a whole crowd of the bad guys with a single turn of her derriere. Crank lifted a conveyor belt full of Madame Gasket's workers into the air and sent them flying off in different directions. Diesel confronted another conveyor belt full of evil bots, knocking them down with his gun as if they were ducks in a shooting gallery.

When the minions approached Piper, she held her nose until her pigtails popped out to the sides, knocking the unsuspecting bots to the ground. Fender kept up a high-pitched scream as he beat one after another bad bot over the head with the battery pack of his electronic prod. He sent at least one flying right over Madame Gasket's head.

In the midst of the commotion, Madame Gasket still had her eye on Bigweld. She snuck over and pulled out the rod that had stopped his cauldron. Madame Gasket couldn't help but smile as she watched the cauldron resume its progress toward the grinder.

But Rodney had seen the cauldron start to move. He was determined to save Bigweld! He used the Wonderbot for a ride up to the cauldron. After giving Rodney a lift, the Wonderbot distracted Madame Gasket by exploding into a cloud of smoke. Madame Gasket began to laugh, but things weren't so funny when the smoke cleared and she saw the new souped-up Wonderbot emerge with spinning tendrils.

While the Wonderbot and Madame Gasket started fighting, Rodney used his wrench to unhook Bigweld's cauldron. Holding onto the chain, Bigweld and Rodney were lifted up into the rafters. Up there they could survey the scene—it didn't look good.

Ratchet was leading the sweepers toward the Rusties. Rodney and Bigweld heard him yell "Lunchtime, boys!" Lug was pushing one of the sweepers, trying to hold it back. Rodney and Bigweld looked around for inspiration. They weren't about to give up.

Rodney spotted a large saw blade hanging from an archway directly above his head. Bigweld's eyes followed Rodney's upward glance. "Are you thinking what I'm thinking?" he asked the young inventor.

"I sure am!" Rodney cried as he released the saw from its support beam. Rodney and Bigweld swung down on the saw toward the sweepers.

"See a need, fill a need!" Rodney yelled to Bigweld as they clung to the blade.

"This isn't what I was thinking at all!" he shouted back.

The pair smashed into the sweepers and were sent flying into a massive pile of junk. One by one, each sweeper fell over, like the dominoes in Bigweld's mansion.

Up above, Madame Gasket and the Wonderbot were still

fighting. Finally, the Wonderbot managed to send Madame Gasket swinging down, out of control, on her harness.

Far below, Ratchet was panicking. He jumped from his fallen sweeper and grabbed blindly at the only thing within his reach. He heard someone scream. "Aah! What are you doing? Get off me!" It was his mother and she was furious. He had clutched onto the hem of her skirt! Together they swung on her harness toward the grinder and narrowly missed. "Let me go! Do as I say! Get off!" she commanded Ratchet. Ratchet, fearing for his life, held tight to the chain. But as they swung again toward the grinder the weight was too much. Snap! The chain broke, catapulting Madame Gasket into the grinder once and for all.

A terrified Ractchet flew up to the ceiling on the remainder of the chain. Within seconds, the evil bot was right where he belonged . . . hanging next to his father from the ceiling of his mother's Chop Shop. Clang! Clunk! Bang! Ratchet's upgrades fell from his body, revealing the skinny weakling within. Now the Rusties and outmodes could see the truth. Beneath the upgrades, Ratchet was no better than they were. In fact, he was worse.

The Rusties looked down at the massive pile of junk beneath their feet. Bigweld and Rodney were nowhere to be seen. Surely, even the toughest bot couldn't survive a crash like that. Just then, Rodney and Bigweld popped their heads from out of the pile. They were alive! Everyone cheered wildly. Piper ran to Rodney and hugged him tight. Cappy waited to hug Rodney, who was truly the bravest bot she had ever met. Everyone was so excited they hardly noticed Madame Gasket, who looked like a pile of crushed metal, coming down the conveyor belt. Bigweld turned to Rodney. "Come on, Rodney. Let's open the gates of Bigweld Industries forever!" But Rodney's mind was somewhere else.

"Wait a minute," he said slowly. "There's one thing I need to do first."

CHAPTER FIFTEEN

News often traveled slowly to Rivet Town, so Herb Copperbottom had no idea what a hero his son had become in the big city. All he knew was that there seemed to be a never-ending supply of dishes coming his way, and he was having more and more trouble keeping up with the younger, newer models of dishwashers out there. Still, the old bot did his best, chugging away as the grease and grime was washed away within his torso.

He looked over at a new pile of dirty dishes and sighed, just as Mrs. Copperbottom walked through the door.

"Herb!" Mrs. Copperbottom said excitedly

"Honey, what are you doing here?" Mr. Copperbottom asked, confused.

"It's Rodney." Mrs. Copperbottom could barely contain herself.

This caught Mr. Copperbottom's attention. "Rodney?!" He repeated his son's name. "Is he all right?"

"Come outside! Hurry!" Was the only answer Mrs. Copperbottom could give him.

Mr. Copperbottom started to follow his wife out when Mr. Gunk barged into the kitchen. "Copperbottom! Where are you going? What about the dishes?"

Rodney's dad didn't know what to say, so instead he unstrapped his dishwasher unit and plunked it onto Mr. Gunk. Now Mr. Gunk could wash all the dishes he wanted.

Mr. Copperbottom had been confused before, but when he stepped out and saw bots celebrating in the streets, he really didn't know what to think. "What is all this?" He asked Mrs. Copperbottom.

A strange bot with a male torso and an attractive set of female legs came up to talk to them, but Mr. Copperbottom was already looking past the bot at a platform set up above the crowd. There, above all the others, Rodney was shaking the hand of none other than Bigweld!

Mr. Copperbottom could barely believe his eyes. And when Rodney introduced him to Bigweld a few minutes later, he was practically speechless.

Fortunately, Rodney's dad didn't need to say much since Bigweld was about to give a speech. "Mr. and Mrs. Copperbottom," he began, "I came all this way to tell you in person, that your son Rodney, the man who got me off my big titanium tuchas, is now my right-hand bot and my eventual successor!"

Mr. Copperbottom looked from his son to Bigweld and back again. "Eventual successor?" he repeated.

Rodney gave his father a huge hug. "Dad, I know you kinda felt bad when I was growing up . . . that you couldn't give me a lot of stuff. But you gave me what I really needed, the most important thing. You believed in me."

Then Rodney handed a strange-looking trumpet to the Wonderbot. "Dad, I know you always wanted to be a musician. Now be one for everyone to hear." The Wonderbot attached the trumpet to Mr. Copperbottom and soon, all of Rivet Town was treated to a sampling of Mr. Copperbottom's musical genius.

Except, Mr. Copperbottom's playing sounded more like a squeaky mistake than any recognizable musical genre. Not wanting to ruin Mr. Copperbottom's moment, Bigweld was gently instructing the band to play along loudly when the Wonderbot flew up using his tendrils to play himself like an old-fashioned washboard.

Somehow, the Wonderbot's playing managed to make sense of Mr. Copperbottom's bizarre trumpet noises. Soon, the whole town was playing along, drumming on whatever they could find.

It was the biggest party Rivet Town had ever seen. Fender was reunited with his girlfriend, Loretta, from the Bigweld Ball, while Rodney and Cappy danced together happily.

But the most triumphant moment was probably when the Wonderbot found Tim, the guard, lurking in the crowd.

He swooped down into the crowd and lifted Tim up into the air.

"Hey, wait a minute!" Tim shouted, as he was ejected from the celebration. "I was on the list! Don't you know who I am? I'm Tim from the TV show."

But the Wonderbot wasn't giving in. Tim was out, Rodney was in. Everything had changed now. The young son of a dish-washer was now the son of a musician. A bad musician, but a musician just the same. Rodney was no longer an outcast, he was a hero. He had friends, he had a girl to call his own, and he was respected everywhere, even here in Rivet Town. And he'd done it all without a single upgrade.

What more could a bot ask for?